I0545716

THE

OLD SANCTUARY.

A ROMANCE OF THE ASHLEY.

BY A. J. REQUIER.

AUTHOR OF THE "SPANISH EXILE," A PLAY, ETC., ETC.

It is the voice of years that are gone!—Ossian.

LONDON:

PUBLISHED BY EDWARD LLOYD, 12, SALISBURY-SQUARE, FLEET-STREET,
AND G. PURKESS, 60, DEAN STREET, SOHO.

THE OLD SANCTUARY.

A ROMANCE.'

THE CONFESSION.

["Oh, injured shade of my departed father," he cried, suddenly dropping upon his knees, and clasping his hands fervently together, "look down upon thy repentant son."]

CHAPTER I.

A heavier task could not have been imposed,
Than I to speak my griefs unspeakable.

Comedy of Errors.

His heart was swoll'n and turned aside
By deep, interminable pride ;
That first, false passion of his breast
Roll'd, like a torrent, o'er the rest.

The Siege of Corinth.

IT was in the year 17—. There stood, at that period, upon the fertile banks of the Ashley, a building, whose rude, gothic structure never failed to excite, at first sight, feelings of astonishment and awe. For years it had been inhabited by the St. Julians—a family originally from France, who emigrated to South Carolina, with many others of their Huguenot brethren, when the government of that country published its sanguinary edict against the exercise of a free conscience, in matters of religious faith. This family was always distinguished by a degree of mingled courtesy and pride, which exhibited a striking, though, perhaps, not unfamiliar contrast to those unacquainted with their character. To their equals, they were generous, but reserved, indifferent, and formal ; to their inferiors, they were humane, yet haughty, arrogant, and supercilious ;—at least, such was the reputation which they had too long and consistently sustained, not to have exhausted all the fountains of good-will and kindliness in the hearts of their neighbours.

A spring evening had set in with its fragrant coolness of breeze, and silvery mellowness of light. Upon a spacious and curiously wrought arm-chair sat an old man, in a room situated in the north-east end of the mansion. A brilliant lamp burnt upon a richly ornamented table near him, and as the wind, entering through the open window, frolicked among his straggling locks of white hair, a lofty brow was revealed, resembling the ivory in softness of polish, and transparency of lustre. He was evidently meditating upon some object of profound interest to his mind. His head reclined upon his right arm ; his eye, darkly shadowed by its long and heavy lashes, was riveted on the fantastic folds that deepened the crimson hue of the damask curtains, and his left hand grasped the arm-chair's seat, with an energy that the expression of his firmly compressed lips explained. The door slowly opened, and a youth entered, without interrupting his reflections. He approached the spot occupied by the old man, and, folding his arms, paused, as if disposed to wait until the latter should awaken from his visible abstraction.

"Edward!" he exclaimed, half starting, as he observed the new comer, a moment after. "How long have you been here ? Why did you not speak?"

"I but this moment came in, and, observing your thoughtful mood, was unwilling to disturb it," answered the youth.

"Tut—tut—you shouldn't mind my reveries—they ought to be familiar to you now. My son, I sent for you—sit down," he added, in a tone of impatience ; "you know that I dislike to speak to a person who is standing—chairs, too, on every side— how you do delight to fret me!"

"Well, father, I am seated," said the other, suiting the action to the word.

"Now," continued the old man, drawing a long breath, as if considerably relieved by the attitude of the person whom he addressed, "I sent for you, Edward, to speak about that fellow Rosalind, and his daughter."

"Blanche, sir—what of her?"

"Blanche, sir—Blanche, indeed!" echoed the elder St. Julian, his eye suddenly turning upon the youth, with a glance at once searching and severe. "You are familiar, sir, it seems, with the name."

"I am acquainted—slightly—acquainted ——"

"No, sir! not slightly acquainted," sternly interrupted his father. "I am old, boy— old in the ways of the world—in its experiences of the heart—the young heart—mistaken at every step, deluded by every flower—blinded by its own sunshine—its guiltless purity of purpose and of speech. I am old, Edward—look at my hair—it is white—is it not? You can impose upon yourself, but not deceive me." As he concldued these observations, his scrutinizing glance was still fixed upon the agitated youth.

"I am acquainted with Miss Rosalind, father," said Edward, endeavouring to conceal his confusion—"nothing more! I am not sensible that other than ordinary good feeling exists on either side; at least, I can safely say so for myself."

"Can you? I am glad of it, my son; she is no match for you."

"She is richer than we are!"

"Granted—she is no match for you."

"And very beautiful!"

"So were her parents," said the old man, bitterly; "still she is no match for you."

"I see not, father," said Edward, somewhat annoyed at the summary manner in which his remonstrances were disposed of—"I see not, father, your reasons for deeming her no match for me; explain yourself."

"Explain myself! I deal not with the lover, sir; I address the son; and shall speak that which implies a command, requiring obedience, not explanation."

Edward St. Julian rose from his seat, with considerable astonishment depicted in his countenance.

"I must confess, sir," he said, "that your language surprises me."

"Does it?" quietly observed his father. "I regret exceedingly that my parental injunctions should conflict with your romantic notions of future felicity. I see, sir," he continued, "that you are very slightly acquainted with the lady, and now fully appreciate your ignorance of a matter in which you are so little interested."

"Nay, father," proudly returned the young man, visibly offended at the equivocation which the other's remarks pointed out, "if you will have me describe the feelings I entertain for Miss Rosalind, I am fully prepared to confirm your suspicion in reference to their character. Though but recently familiar with that lady, I have had many opportunities of witnessing the virtues of her heart. She it was that realized, in all their ideal fulness, my youthful conceptions of the beautiful in nature and the pure in thought. Is it strange, then, that these impressions should have expanded and flowered into passion? Is it unaccountable that I should not have beheld the blending of virtue and beauty, in one being, without experiencing those tender emotions, which your language convinces me you at once anticipate and dread?"

"Ay—ay!" interrupted his father. "I know all you would say—you may have reached the eleventh, but the twelfth hour is yet to come. You must forget the graces of her person, and the qualities of her mind—bury their remembrance in eternal oblivion. The memory, child, should be flexible, when filial devotion is to be tested by its flexibility. I have spoken, and, I trust, we now understand each other."

" And I have spoken, sir."

" What of that ?" eagerly questioned the old man, glancing anxiously at the speaker, who stood erect—his arms folded, and his dark blue eyes earnestly bent upon his father—the picture of offended pride, and cool, though respectful determination.   No answer was returned.

" Edward !" exclaimed the old man, suddenly starting up, and grasping his arm, vehemently, " you do not mean to thwart me.   Boy," he continued, after a slight pause, in a voice of suppressed breathing and intense emotion, " be mindful how you urge parental fondness to extremes—mark me—I am resolved."

" And so am I," fiercely answered the youth.

" On what ?" quickly questioned his father.

" On that which my sense of duty dictates, and yours must also approve, my father.   I have long ago decided that I am responsible to no one for my inclinations, while they flow in the legitimate channels of truth and virtue ; and you know little of my character, if you think that I would tamely submit to an abridgement of those sacred rights, which the humours of a parent should respect.   I have determined, sir, that the partner of my future life—be she humbled or exalted—shall be the subject of my own choice, and having been so chosen, nothing but a conviction of her unworthiness may prompt me to discard her from my affections."

While the young man spoke, his father's countenance exhibited all the varied aspects of contending passion.   His lips quivered—his nostrils dilated—his forehead grew louring and dark, and his feet alternately beat upon the floor the nervous measure of deepening excitement and anger.

At last he broke forth—" Child !" but the effort was too much for his feeble frame, and he fell back upon the seat from which he had temporarily risen, exhausted by the frenzied struggles of his heart.   " I knew it," he tremulously groaned.   " I felt it would come ! Oh, just Heaven ! how certain are thy judgments ! how unfailing thy retributions ! Curse of an injured father ! thy crushing hand still presses me down."

His head dropped heavily upon his breast, and tears brightened, as they swiftly coursed each other down the wrinkles on the old man's cheek.

Moved by his father's agitation, Edward St. Julian approached and gazed upon him with a degree of sorrowing solicitude which spoke eloquently for his filial veneration.

" Father !" he exclaimed, in a subdued and winning voice.

" Who calls me father ?" cried the old man, wildly.   " Yes, I had children once, but all, save one, have died, and he lives to blast the hopes I have garnered up for years—to sunder the bonds which unite us together—so—so—I am childless now."

" Father," cried Edward, touched by his parent's words, " you know me not ! I am hasty—passionate—impulsive, but not heartless.   I mistook your motive—you would not explain it—I was rash ; pardon me—pardon me !"

He took his father's hand as he spoke, and there was a pathos in his manner, which none could have observed without emotion.

" You charge me, Edward," said the elder St. Julian, endeavouring, after a pause, to master his emotion—" you charge me, Edward, with having been ambiguous, in requiring of you the painful sacrifice of your fondest hopes and best affections.   Sit down "—he pointed to a chair—" you shall be satisfied.   I was thus equivocal, my son, because the explanation of my motives involved the recital of a story, which is among the darker pages of my past history.   You are young, and therefore cannot well conceive how trying ¹t is to the heart, which has, for years, severely bled, to unwind the stubborn springs of guilt, and injury, and despair, intermingled by a cruel fate, with its foreboding thoughts and feverish dreams. May Providence, in its infinite mercy, spare you the terrible experience! Bear with me a moment, while I recall to my scattered senses, and recite the lengthy catalogue of woe, which whitened ·my head ere the frost of age had weakened my limbs, and the tempest of my young and headstrong passions had subsided into the calm of a deep, but voiceless grief." He paused to wipe the liquid traces of his recent tears, and thus continued.—" My father, though disinterested and noble, was a haughty, overbearing man. Born in the plentiful lap, and educated in the obstinate wilfulness, of wealth, he knew little of the cares of want, and less of the anxietudes of disappointment. Restless and passionate in temper and inclination, he commanded with strength, and ruled with severity. I grew up beneath his eye, and insensibly added to the evil passions I inherited with my blood, the more pernicious habits of thought and action by which they had been strengthened in his mind. Our feelings ran parallel, and constant jarring was thus produced between us. It seemed the delight of his wayward disposition to thwart all my schemes and expectations. Oh! woe be unto him, my son, who, being familiar with a parent's vices, lacks the discriminating prudence and soul-exalting energy to profit by the melancholy example. Alas! I had neither. At an early age, I loved ; and the object of my passion belonged to a family who were humbly dependent ‘on my sire for subsistence. There was the distance of the poles between us—and I saw it ; yet the blind infatuation of my feelings overlooked the chasm and reconciled the contrariety. My excited imagination persuaded me to declaim against the wise distinctions of society, and to denounce its prejudices as uncalled for and despotic. It was the philosophy of Love, and I believed in its truth with the enthusiastic devotion of a saint. Vision of folly! who had told me then I should one day be a martyr ? There was a man, with whom I had grown up, and to whom I was attached by the strongest ties of friendship. Our fathers had been intimate before us ; and in the belief of his sincerity, I confided to him all the circumstances of my unfortunate predilection. He coincided in all my extravagant plans, approved of all my thoughtless indiscretions, and his advice served only to enliven the flame which burnt but too intensely in my bosom. Finally, I determined to declare my sentiments to my father, and either to win his consent, or to set his opposition at defiance. This was cruel ; for he was old and infirm— tottering on the verge of his grave—and I might have waited for nature to perform the work, which my parricidal hand did not shudder to accomplish. Be that as it may!

" The day for the denouement was appointed. It came. My father was afflicted with the return of a periodical disease, and the attack was, this time, unusually severe. I would have delayed the consummation of my project, but my friend" — a frown darkened the old man's brow,—" my friend, I say, urged me to be firm—conclude what I had dared to commence. I waited on my father. It was towards evening. The aged invalid sat upon a chair " —— here the speaker examined that upon which he was seated, and a slight tremor might have been observed, as he continued, "the same—the very same! His brow, naturally stern and repulsive, wore a soft and subdued expression, as if the pains of disease had humbled the proud man to a sense of his comparative insignificance. He greeted me with unwonted cordiality ; but his gentleness affected me not. I was wild—frenzied with the ungovernable longings of an ardent passion—anticipating obstacles, and resolved to trample them under foot. Vesuvius was in my heart ; its yawning furnace ready to engulph the victim—consuming waters heaving against the barriers which arrested their destructive progress. I spoke to him—the author of my life—my aged, dying father—words! words! Oh, such words! Reason, my son, had lost its sway—her barren sceptre was on the earth; I had drained the gall and hyssop to its very dregs; I was mad—mad to agony!" The speaker's voice, stifled and broken by his emotions, sank almost to a whisper, as he resumed. "He remonstrated—this proud, haughty, unyielding spirit—this giant of pride, remonstrated with me. It was all in vain—the avalanche was roaring on its impetuous course! I heeded not; but scoffed—upbraided—ridiculed—scorned him! God! that I should live to speak it. He stood up—the death-stricken patriarch stood up;—his voice, like the pealing thunders of Heaven, rung in my ears, as it imprecated its vengeance on my head; and a father's curse was graven eternally on my vicious heart, as he staggered and fell, bathed in his blood, upon the floor—his ghastly eyeballs fixed, in life's last, agonizing struggles, on the murderer—his only child—his once beloved son! Edward, thou hast heard the worst—I was a wretch—a heartless, miserable wretch;—yet, in pity, scorn me not, my child! my child!"

The aged father wrung his hands in bitterness, and clung convulsively around the young man's neck, while big tears rolled thick and fast down his pale and colourless cheek.

"Speak no more, my father," said Edward, imploringly. "The effort is too much for your debilitated frame; another time—we have all our cross of affliction to bear, and with some it is heavier than others."

"Edward!" exclaimed the old man, pressing him closer to his throbbing breast, "thou speakest words of consolation. And wilt thou never desert me, then? He said the joys of my life would wither, one by one, and so they have! Thy mother sleeps in her grave, thy brothers are no more—thou art all that is left me now. Oh, injured shade of my departed father," he cried, suddenly dropping upon his knees, and clasping his hands fervently together, "look down on thy repentant son. The cup of his sorrow and wailing overflows! Recall—in mercy recall the curse that thou didst wreak upon his sinful head—annul the decree, which condemns him to die ' forlorn and forsaken, in the tenantless halls of his fathers!'"

Edward St. Julian gazed, in speechless horror, upon the terrible example of guilt and remorse which stood before him. Overcome by the exertions he had made, the unfornate man still retained the attitude in which his passionate invocation had thrown him. The reciprocally energetic grasp of his hands, which had fallen united to his knees, was partially relaxed, and his eyes, half closed, struggled mournfully with their heavy lids, as if striving to look upwards. With that morbid acuteness of perception, which, when fancy and feeling are aroused, occasions our forcing every circumstance which may contribute to the latter's excitement, into the former's still expanding circle, the young man shuddered at the doleful moanings of the wind without, which came mingled with the swamp-bird's piercing shriek, in painfully protracted notes upon his ear.

But these gloomy imaginings were not of long duration. Mastering them with the vigour of a nicely balanced intellect, he proceeded to offer his grief-stricken parent such poor consolations as the discomposure of his own mind afforded.

"I am resigned, my son," said the elderly man, rising, and reseating himself with the youth's assistance. "I am resigned to my fate. It is the will of Heaven; and I bow to it, in meekness and humility."

But vainly did Edward attempt to dissuade him from continuing the sad story that he had commenced.

"No," he replied to all his solicitations, "you must hear the sequel. I have related the history of my guilty infatuation and rashness; you must now learn that of my wrongs. Wrongs, my son, which thy heart should burn, and thine arm tremble, to avenge!"

A deep and unaccountable sadness crept over the young man's spirits while listening to these words; and he felt a rising impediment in his throat, as he nodded an assent, which his tongue involuntarily refused to speak.

The speaker continued,—

"For several days previous to that on which occurred the fatal catastrophe I have described, I had observed that my friend was constantly closeted with my father. Though I naturally experienced some curiosity to learn the subject of their private conferences, motives of false delicacy made me refrain from questioning my companion as to their character. The death and consequent publicity of my father's will but too amply attested the villanous part he sustained in their secret consultation. By the tenour of that instrument, all the property over which the deceased exercised absolute control, was entailed upon my pretended friend and his posterity. However, had his villany stopped here, I might have pardoned him; but it went farther—too far for human forbearance, or christian forgiveness. He seduced—ah, you may well shrink—basely seduced, the woman for whom I had braved the frown and curses of a dying father—staked and for ever lost the future peace of my soul. Oh! my son, learn from my fatal example this important lesson—and see that you bear it unviolated to the tomb. True felicity consists in the constant and undeviating practice of virtue; and that object, which promises happiness as a reward for its sacrifice, is but an *ignis fatuus*, which allures the storm-tossed wanderer of life, only to mislead him from his path. You may wonder that I allowed myself to be so greatly deceived. Alas! what inexperienced and confiding mind can fathom the depths of that deception, which wears a smile upon the lip, to conceal the deep-dyed blackness of the heart. Suffice it, I was deceived; bitterly, cruelly, basely deceived! Rendered desperate by the foul injuries I had suffered, I would have immolated their author to my blasted prospects and ruined hopes; but, with a villain's hardihood, he lacked a ruffian's courage, and speedily fled with the wretch he had fascinated to betray. Years rolled on in their uninterrupted course, and I lived a confirmed misanthrope—a burden to others and to myself. I hated the world, contemned its pleasures, despised its philosophy. Fate at last threw into my desolate path a woman who united to a combination of the most brilliant attractions, a soul whose virtues were unsurpassed. She subdued and softened my proud and scornful heart, till its long pent-up sympathies and affections freely circulated in the living sepulchre, where they had been congealed and frozen. I loved her; but it was not a morning, not a meridian glow. We married —were blessed with beautiful offspring, and, for a time, felt cheerful and happy. Alas! it was an April sunshine, and its evanescent beams could not defeat the dark-winged prophecy which hovered over my head. One by one my children died—thou alone, my Edward, remained; and the first effort of thy infant limbs was to totter in the sad procession which followed thy dead mother's bier. What has since transpired thou knowest —*all*, now, is told."

"No!" exclaimed Edward, "one thing is yet untold. The villain—where is *he*?"

"Here," quickly responded his father; "here, within my reach, with his ill-gotten gold glistening in my face, and his liveried minions eager to defend a life, which he is too cowardly to risk, and I have too much virtue left to extinguish by crime."

"His name?"

"What would you? Vengeance may be tardy, but it is certain."

"Be it so! His name?"

" It is vain. You can—you dare do nothing," expostulated his father.

" I dare do all things to revenge an injured parent's wrongs!" The blood alternately came and went in the young man's cheek, and his lips quivered as he spoke.

" Swear it, then !" cried the old man.

" I do," solemnly replied the other. At this moment, the lamp's vivid flame, streaming unsteadily along a sudden current of wind, that entered through the open lattice, was gradually extinguished ; and the moonlight revealed the speaker's face, haggard and pale as death.

" The oath is registered," said the father, a look of triumph darting from his sunken eyes. Then, grasping the young man's arm, he bent forward, and whispered, in smothered and low, but startlingly audible tones—" Philip Rosalind !"

A cry of intense anguish broke from the youth, and he rushed wildly from the apartment.

CHAPTER II.

When with greatest art he spoke,
You'd think he talk'd like other folk.—Hudibras.

WITHIN fifty miles of St. Julian Mansion, no one doubted,—for no one could doubt,—the schoolmaster's vainglorious self-complacency and importance—Timothy Shaftsbury Twiddle ; a designation to which his warmer admirers invariably subjoined the flattering adjunct—Esquire. The extent of his learning, however, was quite another question, and therefore admitted a variety of conflicting opinions. Some declared him skilled in those mystic languages, which add so much to the blockhead's vanity, if not to the scholar's usefulness ; others described him as profound in the principles of natural and speculative science—while a secret and sacrilegious few were known openly to ridicule and contemn his proverbial temerity and professional dogmatism. But his benevolence, by a single act of apparently disinterested generosity, had been redeemed from all the disparaging influences of disputation. So, as the world went, though some thought him a Falstaff, and others a philosopher—this one a ninny, and that one a Newton—all were agreed on the uncomplimentary point, that he was, beyond all controversy, a very good-natured sort of a somebody. Now, Timothy Shaftsbury was not remarkable only for the great diversity of opinion which the natural character of his brain, and the peculiar character of its furniture, excited. There were other singularities about him. The conformation of his cranium was singular ; it was quite as unshapely as the three-cornered hat which adorned it. His hair was singular ; it stuck out like the whalebone props of an Englishman's family umbrella, besides being grey on week days, and changeable black on Sunday. His eyes were singular ; they looked for all the world as if they intended to jump out, and take a ride upon his huge proboscis, which, singular in its steep ascent and sudden declivity, seemed desirous of annoying, by its disagreeable vincinage, a mouth that closed with as much neatness of wrinkle as an old maid's work-bag, and was, therefore, deemed very singular too. But more amusing than all his other oddities was Timothy's dress. He wore a long black coat, which, like that of the old gentleman in the misery ballad, was " all buttoned down before." The well-starched and pointed sides of his shirt collar grew out of a tall white cravat, which was lost to the sight in a voluminous bed of ruffles that protruded from his breast in all manner of fantastic twists and turns. His knee-breeches, once of a dark snuff-colour, had turned to a dingy amalgamation of multifarious

THE SAD MELTING IN THE SANCTUARY.

[Edward's head rested upon his arm, and an air of deep despondency overspread his handsome features. "Edward!" she anxiously exclaimed. No answer was returned.]

hues, more easily seen than described; and, "last, but not least," his shoes were high quartered, and ornamented with shining steel buckles, which, as honest tradition reported, had been worn by his great-great-grandfather, Sir Ignatius Twiddle, Bart. Such was Timothy Shaftsbury Twiddle, a gentleman of more extended notoriety than genuine learning, and much less charity than cunning.

"Silence!" exclaimed the schoolmaster, entering a little outhouse, whose location was contiguous to that of his dwelling, and casting a glance fully as authoritative as that of a Russian autocrat at a handful of shabby-looking boys who were buzzing over their morning lessons. Then, walking up to his elevated seat, he applied the tip end of his ferula to the tip end of his nose, and proceeded to scrutinise the surrounding urchins with the searching penetration of an Argus.

"Smikes, stop sneezing—little boys should not sneeze." This was addressed to a sickly-complexioned lad in the corner, who had been repeating the offensive physical effort alluded to for several minutes past. "Smikes, I begin to believe it was you that stole my Scotch snuff. I'd like to know," he continued, looking around him, "who scratched that Julius Cæsar off my snuffbox,—I'd give him Julius Cæsar! Jenks, stop making faces like Mrs. Tuitrac. Swiggins, come here." This was addressed to a third, who approached with a deferential trembling of the limbs. "Your father wouldn't pay me the quarter's schooling this morning. Do you know what the Scriptures say on that subject?"

"No, no, sir!" stuttered the boy.

"The sins of the parent," answered Mr. Twiddle, elevating his ruler as he spoke, "shall be visited upon the child to the third and fourth generations. You belong to the first; open your hand."

Here the dose of punishment adequate to the offence was administered, and the delinquent sent squealing to his seat.

"Study that geography, you rogue," he cried, to a lively-faced youth opposite him. "You think I didn't hear you call me a dirty blackguard name yesterday. Eh! if I were only sure it was your voice!"

This threat was accompanied by a shake of the lash, full of terrible significance and meaning.

"I never called you 'Jingle Timothy,' sir," remonstrated the boy.

"Say that again, you unmannerly brute!" cried the schoolmaster, standing up from his chair, and stepping towards the speaker; "repeat that horrid expression—do it— and I'll break every bone in your body. You fight biddies again?" he abruptly exclaimed, striking a little fellow who sat next to the other sharply on the head, as if determined that his anger should be expended indiscriminately upon all.

Just at this moment, a head, covered with all kinds of lace-work and ribbons, was thrust into the door.

"Teminy! Teminy!" softly called Mrs. Twiddle, for it was she. He paid no attention to the call. "Shaftsbury!" repeated the same voice, but in a somewhat harsher key. Again no answer was returned. "Mr. Twiddle!" vociferated his amiable lady, "haven't you no ears?"

"Yes, my dear," quickly responded the individual addressed, who knew the danger of overlooking the third summons. "Really, my dear,—I didn't hear you, my dear; these boys annoy me so."

"You are wanted in the house," gruffly observed his partner.

"Am I?" blandly ejaculated her husband.

" Yes, you are, my dear," the wife echoed, mockingly, adding in her usual pettish tone, " and the sooner you go the better." In obedience to the lady's injunction, Mr. Twiddle turned upon his high heel, and walked towards the house. " Boys," she said, addressing his pupils, " Mr. Twiddle is engaged;—you may all have holiday to-day." Then, following her husband, she left the school-room, in one general uproar of boyish hilarity and glee.

Upon entering the apartment where his guest was seated, the schoolmaster assumed a superlatively gracious expression of countenance, and bowed very obsequiously as he repeated his usual salutation, " Happy to see you, sir!—very happy to see you, sir!—exceedingly happy to see you, sir!" The stranger nodded in return.

" My name, Mr. Twiddle," he commenced, " is Rosalind."

" Rosalind!" ejaculated the schoolmaster, starting up in amazement at the joyful conviction of having a landholder in his house. " I am delighted, sir!—I am quite delighted, sir!—I am exceedingly delighted, sir!—won't you dine with me?"

A keen observer would perhaps have detected a little *hauteur* in the stranger's voice, as he readily declined the unexpected invitation; but there was too much suavity artfully intermixed with it, to warrant a suspicion, in the other's mind, that his offer had excited other than the most agreeable emotions. As for the offer itself, it had been rather a subject of amusement than surprise, to those who boasted of any acquaintance with Mr. Twiddle's character. All men, more or less, however narrow-minded and egotistical, wear the semblance of some generous impulse to conceal their selfishness; and this was the screen which a naturally convivial disposition had, perhaps, originally suggested to the schoolmaster, and habit subsequently confirmed into a distinguishing peculiarity.

Gradually composing his features to their original gravity and sternness, he prepared to hear his guest.

" You must know, Mr. Twiddle," the other began, " that I have a daughter, who, like all young girls of her age, has taken a love crotchet into her head. I have every reason to believe that the object of her girlish fancy is young St. Julian."

" I never liked those St. Julians," interrupted Timothy, with an ominous shake of the hear.

Rosalind bowed slightly, and continued—" Though, of late, I have employed every expedient that coercion dictated to prevent any intercourse between them, they have succeed in baffling all my plans, and repeatedly met each other in secret."

" Ah!" cried Mr. Twiddle, who, though little interested as yet, thought an exclamation indispensable to good breeding.

" Well—as I was about to observe," resumed the visitor, " all these secret interviews were, I am credibly informed, managed by a little girl, who resides with you."

" Oh! little black-eyed Nora, you mean—very probably, very probably, sir," remarked the schoolmaster.

" I do not know her name. Indeed, I have never seen her; for I am so seldom out of my dwelling that I have no opportunity of becoming familiar with the faces of my neighbours," answered Rosalind. " But my information is based upon the authority of a person whose veracity I have never had occasion to suspect. Now—Mr. Twiddle—if you could turn this little creature adrift ——"

" As for that matter," gravely interfered the schoolmaster, " I would hardly like to say. She is very useful to Mrs. Twiddle, and though a poor foundling—yet, having grown up under our roof, we feel some sort of an affection for the child. So, you observe, Mr. Rosalind, I shouldn't like to undertake the setting her adrift as you propose."

"Hear me out," resumed the other, earnestly. "Blanche's nurse has repeatedly endeavoured to win the girl over to our side—and, as often, signally failed. I have something at stake in this matter, and am convinced that the measure proposed is the only one which may be successfully employed to defeat these young people. If money——"

"Really, sir," said Timothy, smiling peculiarly, "really, sir, I didn't observe the unavoidable necessity of your expedient before; I say, being ignorant that you had tried other means—you understand—these things taken together persuade me to promise, that—that——" Here his eyes swam, for they rushed upon two notes of £100 each, which Rosalind had taken from his purse.

"No, I understand you," remarked the latter, a sardonic smile playing around his lips; "and, doubtless, you understand me."

During the pause which ensued, at this important stage of their conversation, a young girl, of apparently some twelve or thirteen summers, entered the room. Her appearance, remarkable in the extreme, was eminently calculated to interest the beholder. She was rather below the height usually attained by those of her age. Her limbs, which seemed fragile to a fault, were yet exquisitely moulded, and gracefully proportioned. Her eyes were of a jet black hue, and as she rolled their large and pensively languid orbs around, there was a strange fascination about them, which enchained the attention as a magic spell. But the effect produced by their singular darkness (which, united to her unusually short stature, had obtained for her the universal appellation of "Little Black-eyed Nora,") was doubtless considerably increased by a delicate rosy tinge upon her cheeks, and the shining whiteness of her brow and neck, with which they vividly contrasted. Elegant ringlets of glossy black hair hung in massive clusters around the last, almost concealing it from the view, save where a plain ebony cross, suspended upon her slightly rounded breast, arrested the eye, as if to check its sinful fancies, which its budding charms might have excited.

Rosalind's back being turned to the door, the maiden was consequently unobserved by him at first; but as she advanced towards the schoolmaster, his glance was naturally attracted to her countenance, and he started up pallid and trembling from his seat.

For several minutes he gazed upon her in speechless amazement and terror, and his thin lips, pale and quivering with unaccountable emotions, moved and muttered inaudible sounds.

"No! no! it is not she—nothing!" he exclaimed in somewhat clearer tones, passing his hand slowly across his brow, as if awakening from a dream. Then, making a sufficiently visible effort to recover his lost composure, he said, with a constrained and ghastly smile to the schoolmaster, whose astonishment, hardly excelled by that of the trembling girl, was legibly written upon his features, "You must deem me singular—but the young lady resembles—a friend—a sister—who has been long dead—and—and——" his eyes involuntarily rested again upon the maiden, and, with a shudder, he beckoned her to retire.

"Leave the room!" growled Mr. Twiddle, who began to doubt the evidence of his senses, and was rather uncertain whether he stood upon his head or his heels.

"Is she gone?" anxiously inquired his guest, who appeared unwilling to look in her direction.

"Yes, sir," was the laconic reply.

"Very strange coincidence, this!" observed Rosalind, the same ghastly smile lighting up his features. "I am quite interested, Mr. Twiddle, in your young protege. Pray, how did you come by her?"

The individual addressed drew a long breath, and after unceremoniously scrutinizing his visitor's countenance, to convince himself that he was not a lunatic, in which case, being dreadfully afraid of such people, the schoolmaster intended to leave politeness to take care of itself, and to test the discretion of his legs, he replied,—

"She was left with us when quite a child, by her mother, a crazy woman ——"

"She is not dead, then?" cried Rosalind, with another start, almost as violent as the first.

"I—don't—don't know!" returned Timothy, his teeth chattering for very fear, and quite convinced, by this decided symptom, of the truth of his former suspicion. "Just excuse me, until I drink some water," he added, cautiously approaching the door, and conceiving he could already see the wild glare of insanity in his visitor's eyes.

"Stop!" cried Rosalind, observing his movements, and guessing at the motives which prompted them. "I am calm; you need apprehend no danger from me. I have reasons—reasons which you could not divine, and would hardly believe, for my mysterious looks and actions."

Thus reassured, the schoolmaster returned to his seat; not, however, without giving three or four incredulous glances at the speaker, to be certain that he was really in his senses.

Being desired by his strange guest to continue the maiden's history, which the latter himself had abruptly broken off, he thus continued: "Her mother—as I was saying—appeared bent upon our keeping her, and being happy to get rid of her—for she was a terrible creature, sir; actually killed Mrs. Twiddle's favourite tabby cat with a stone you would scarcely believe a poor thing like her could lift up—being happy to get rid of her at any price, we took the child, and——"

"Enough!—enough!" abruptly interrupted the other. "You have promised to do my bidding?"

The schoolmaster bowed.

"We may meet again," he added, glancing at him significantly. Then, moving towards the door, he almost immediately disappeared.

For several minutes after the stranger's departure, Mr. Twiddle remained in the same position upon his chair, wrapped up in the most heterogeneous mass of unsatisfactory reflections concerning his singular conduct and the occurrence which had evidently produced it. To do him justice, he felt some curiously painful sensations about throwing the poor young orphan, friendless and unprotected, upon a cold world; but these benevolent emotions had no sooner intruded into his heart, than the two notes, which, in the agitation of his feelings, had been dropped upon the floor and there forgotten, suddenly met his eye, and dissipated every other idea, except that of possessing them, from his mind.

"It's a hard thing to do," he soliloquised, stooping down to recover them—"yet, two hundred pounds! think of that, Timothy. She's very young—poh! no child of mine—no blood of the Twiddles. Two hundred pounds! she must go—I'd give my school—my beadleship—ay, Mrs. Twiddle to boot, for two hundred pounds!"

Thus saying, the schoolmaster betook himself to a staircase that conducted into his wife's chamber, determined to apprize her of the unexpected good fortune which was suddenly placed within his reach, and the inhuman act he had consented to perform for its attainment.

CHAPTER III.

And wilt thou leave me thus,
Who lov'd thee hath so long,
Both weal and woe among?
And is thy heart so strong,
As for to leave me thus?
Say nay—say nay !—WYATT.

AT a short distance from the elegant and costly mansion which Rosalind had recently built, were to be seen the dilapidated remnants of what was probably once a family vault. Had its history been susceptible of investigation, its origin would, doubtless, have been ascribed to the primitive settlers of that section of the country. But this was a matter in which the people who inhabited the vicinity were very slightly, if at all, concerned. It was sufficient for them, that the appearance of the ruin afforded the surest evidence of its antiquity, and their dismal fancies were as industriously exerted to invest its natural sombreness with the darker shades of superstitious awe, as their idle tongues were diligent in circulating the mysterious tales by which that object was sought to be effected. Innumerable were the stories which their fireside gossips related concerning this gloomy spot. Heroes of passion, and heroes of strife, were unceremoniously mingled, in these amusing narrations, with enormous giants and wonderful fairies, who contrasted with the fascinating manners and magnanimous prowess of the former, all that crime dared to compass, or that supernatural power could accomplish. Credulous maidens might be found who solemnly protested to have often seen frightful bands of fantastic apparitions prowling at twilight in the surrounding woods, and many were the equally credulous youths who seriously swore they had stumbled on these itinerant spirits in their evening rambles through the fields. With such a reputation, it will be scarcely a subject of surprise, that the Sanctuary (it was so called) was never visited, save by adventurous strangers, whose curiosity was rather enlivened than depressed by these improbable relations. Blanche Rosalind was of the latter. Thither in moments of melancholy reverie she had, at first, frequently resorted, to enjoy, unobserved, the rare luxury of undisturbed solitude; and when her father openly declared his averseness to her lover, and employed every artifice to effect their separation, she discovered another quality in its romantic seclusion, which had never before suggested itself to her mind.

On the morning in which little black-eyed Nora intruded upon the schoolmaster and his guest, she had conveyed to the latter's fair daughter a letter from Edward St. Julian, in which he warmly solicited the favour of an interview.

To the Sanctuary, accordingly, the young lady repaired, with palpitating heart and tremulous step, at the time appointed in her lover's billet.

She sat upon a massive fragment of the monument which had fallen to the ground. Around her the unroofed and broken walls, spotted here and there with sickly weeds or clustering ivy, appeared to frown upon their long and gradually receding shadows. And near the remains of a crumbling portico a solitary rose-tree grew up in wild but rich luxuriance, as if to embody the familiar antithesis of beauty blooming in dreariness of desolation. Blanche had plucked one of these flowers, and she held it almost mechanically in her left hand, which reposed carelessly upon her lap, while the other feebly grasped an angle projecting from the rude seat which she occupied. Her body, though partially bent forward, yet retained all its characteristic grace, and her soft blue eyes were turned with the meekness of habitual devotion to Heaven. The extreme fairness of her complexion—the deep thoughtfulness of her features—the snowy whiteness of her thin garment, which floated like a cloud around her form—all contributed to impart a seraphic expression to her countenance; and her image, reflected in a little rivulet, which, flowing with glassy smoothness at her feet, was lost in the adjacent shrubbery, resembling that of a fountain nymph or sylvan goddess.

She had remained there but a short time, when a sharp noise, as of branches impatiently torn and thrust aside, attracted her attention, and was immediately followed by the handsome figure of Edward St. Julian emerging from an exuberant growth of underwood, that girdled the sequestered vault.

"Blanche!" he said, approaching her with a constrained smile — "dear Blanche, thanks—thanks for this kindness; I scarce expected to find you."

"You scarce expected me, Edward, to violate again the positive injunctions of my father. The thought was charitable—you see I do not deserve it." She spoke these words in a tone of singular sadness, and gazed earnestly up into his face.

"What of his injunctions—who heeds them?" abruptly returned the youth.

"I should, Edward," she eagerly replied, "I should heed them. Alas! I have vainly prayed for the strength to resist an inclination, which I fear eventually will be my ruin."

"Your ruin, Blanche?" he echoed in astonishment—"explain yourself."

"What shall I explain?" exclaimed the maiden. "Know you not my father's unalterable determination? Know you not that he has forbidden me to speak—nay, more," she faltered, "to see you? Edward, she who once turns a deaf ear to the rigid dictates of duty, makes the first and most dangerous advance towards ruin. It is true he has never bestowed upon me those small but endearing attentions which, in some, serve to mark the extent of parental affection, and thus to strengthen the sacred links that bind them to their children: yet, he is my father, and doubtless cherishes his child with an ardour, which is, perhaps, the more intense, because it is concealed. There are minds that seldom display their gentler emotions."

"Ay—there are minds that seldom experience such emotions," bitterly interrupted the young man.

"But he does," quickly returned the young lady. "Else, why has not the culture of my mind been neglected? Why have I unceasingly enjoyed all the luxuries that give unto affluence its exaggerated worth? Why have all my caprices been unsparingly indulged—my childish conceits been gratified?"

"And think you, then, it is the duty of a parent to cater to the wanton fancies of his offspring?" inquired Edward.

"No; I do not. I mention these things merely as illustrative of the blind extravagance of parental affection, which, experience convinces us, is seldom graduated by the nicer scales of sober reflection and calculating propriety. The deep-seated passions of the heart cannot always boast the mild precepts of reason for their guide." The young lady slightly coloured, for her sensitive mind conceived how justly the suggestion applied to herself.

"That is true, Blanche—very true," remarked her lover, with unaffected seriousness. The sincerity and earnestness of manner with which these words were uttered, could not but strike the maiden, and she cast a hurried glance at the speaker. His head rested upon his arm, and an air of deep despondency overspread his handsome and expressive features.

"Edward!" she anxiously exclaimed. No answer was returned. The hitherto subdued expression of his countenance was visibly changing, under the influence of his passing thoughts, to that of mingled agitation and anguish.

"Edward!" she repeated, somewhat terrified by these sudden manifestations of mental disquietude and pain. "You are ill?"

"No, dearest," he quickly replied; "I—am—better. Blanche," he resumed, after a brief interval, with considerable emotion, "it is useless longer to conceal the cause of my sorrow from you. We must part—for ever."

"Part!" cried the girl, and her cheeks grew unearthly pale. "Why, Edward—why should we part?"

"Be calm, dearest," said her lover, soothingly, observing her deep emotion. "I have a story to tell which may explain my meaning. I heard it in my younger days :—listen. The argument was of two men who had grown up in the strictest intimacy and friendship. One of these was a villain. He betrayed his friend into the bewildering paths of vice and passion—called upon him the anathemas of a dying father—seduced the woman whom he loved to madness—would have even taken his life, had not cowardly apprehensions restrained his ruthless arm. They separated; years elapsed ere they again met one another; each was on the opposite road. The vicissitudes of the circle were experienced; and after travelling it through, they stood, once more, at the diverging point. The injured man had a son—a son, in whom all his earthly affections were centered; and this son, though he loved the other's daughter to desperation, swore to avenge his parent's wrongs."

"Well," exclaimed Blanche.

"He did so," continued the youth; "was he not right?"

"I—I—yes," she incoherently replied. The surrounding objects danced before her eyes.

"Then he wooed the daughter," slowly and emphatically returned Edward. "How think you *she* acted? Mark you—he was her father's murderer—his hands were stained with the blood which flowed in her veins—the blood that had given her life. What would you have done?"

"Rejected—spurned him!" fervently exclaimed the indignant maiden.

"You have decided—we part for ever—farewell!" said the youth, starting up violently from his place beside her.

"No—no—Edward!" sobbed the girl, clinging convulsively to his arm. "You are not the man. This is a scheme—a device to try my affection. This tale is the coinage of your own brain. Speak to me! say it is so. Nay, this is ungenerous. You would not break a poor, weak woman's heart."

"Blanche Rosalind, I have sworn it."

His arm was dropped. A moment she paused, resting against the ruined wall for support; then, after several fruitless endeavours to catch her respiration, answered, "I mistook you, sir—be it so—farewell!"

Thus saying, she moved away, and had already reached the ruined portico, when a wild sob fell upon her ear. She turned and gazed upon him. The strong man was overcome, and tears asserted the heart's pre-eminence.

"And is it thus you leave me, Blanche," he said, "without a word at parting? Well, you may go. Do not mind my tears. I am but human flesh and blood—not stone—not stone!"

Moved by these words, which she mistook for indications of repentance and sorrow, the maiden approached him and spoke,—

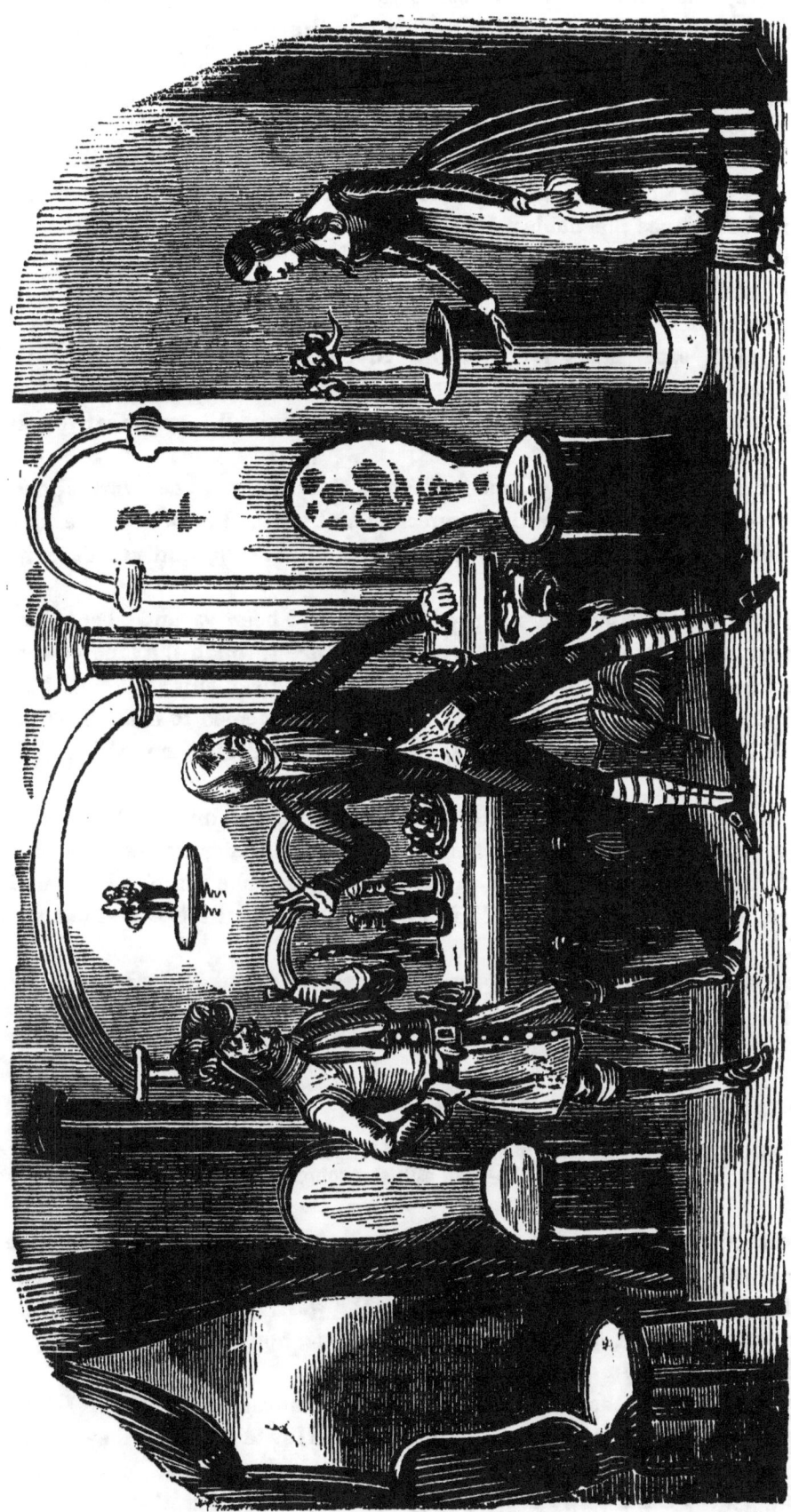

BLANCHE'S UNEXPECTED APPEARANCE TO THE STRANGER.

[The door slowly opened, and Blanche stood musingly at the threshold, undecided whether to advance or recede.]

"Dear Edward," she said, "I am not lost to you. There is yet a remedy. Promise to disregard the cruel obligations of that sinful oath. Promise—faithfully promise to do this, and in spite of all this will I be yours, or never wed another. Do you not love me?" she inquired, persuasively.

"Miss Rosalind," he answered, in a voice hoarse with emotion, "I loved you with all the unfathomable depth, the all-absorbing fervour of adoration. More than all things else— ay, though it be sacrilegious to speak it—the Deity excepted, in the heavens or the earth. For you I would renounce the noblest blessings of life—its gold—its honours—its ambition. Even the loss of freedom would I calmly bear, and the prison's iron-grated cell inhabit for thy sake, with its agonizing privations and withering infamy—its sleepless weariness and frenzied imaginings—its corrupting dampness and corroding chains, would, to my eyes, seem fairer far than all the splendours of a Parian pile, ungilded by thy smile. Ask for these—whatever fortune, talent, birth, connexion, may bestow; head and heart and hand dare grasp at and attain; all! save that uncancelled oath—it is inviolably sacred!"

"All is over!" she despairingly groaned. "Edward St. Julian, your work of desolation has commenced—the happiness of a life is wrecked and gone. Farewell!" she continued; and he imagined he heard a half stifled sob. "I cannot leave, and yet dare not forgive you."

Raising his eyes from the ground upon which they had been vacantly bent during the maiden's speech, he had scarce noticed her disappearance through the tangled shrubbery that obstructed the ivy-grown porch, when a child's voice near him awakened his attention, and speedily turning in the direction from whence it seemed to come, he discovered little Nora, half hid by a moss-covered fragment of the building on which she partly reclined.

"You won't love her any more!" cried the child, looking up innocently into his face, and smiling like sunshine through her tears; then, as if apprehensive that the selfish joy she had manifested would be attributed to its real cause, she clasped her small white hands together, and said, imploringly, "You mustn't scold little Nora—I am wicked— very wicked!"

He gazed upon the little orphan in speechless amazement and compassion.

CHAPTER IV.

Her bosom heav'd with melancholy swell,
And still she turn'd—and still she sobb'd, farewell!

ANONYMOUS.

HAVING reached the top of the staircase, Mr. Twiddle slowly opened the door and entered. He found his gentle consort seated near a window, situated on the left hand side of her diminutive chamber, and confronting the west, quietly enjoying a refreshing breeze which blew from that quarter; while her coarse, bony fingers diligently plied a variety of knitting needles, in contradictory directions.

"Timmy, my dear," said the lady, with unusual pleasantness of accent, "I have just been thinking of the Picknsniffes and Chinchillys. How astonished they'll be to see me next Sunday at church with my stockings! Oh, if I only had a gold necklace, now—a sparkling gold chain to wear round my neck, how put out they'd all be, to be sure, eh?"

Mr. Twiddle signified his unconditional assent to the truth of her observation, by his usual nod.

"Curse that school of yours, Mr. Twiddle!" she continued, somewhat more sharply—"it gives you nothing. There you are trying to beat something into those mop-heads and dunces, the whole live-long day, and their parents give you no thanks, and precious little money. There must be a revolution, Mr. Twiddle; things won't do; they can't continue so; you are too good-natured; the boys must be whipped more severely, sir,—their fathers must pay for it—and I must have a necklace, Mr. Twiddle!"

"Anything, my dear—anything to please you," quickly responded the obliging and timid husband.

"Ay, Mr. Twiddle—you say so—but that's nothing, sir—you must do so. Miss Katharina Picksniff is going to get new slippers, and I ought to have a pair, sir—you must whip the boys. Miss Euphrosina Picksniff has bought a silk gown, with an elegant lace tippet—Mr. Twiddle, the boys must be scored. Then there's that pert-faced, hump-nosed Chinchilly girl, she's going to wear the fashion, too—what I can't wear—Mr. Twiddle, I'll be the death of you if you don't be the death of the boys!"

"Don't be so nervous, my love," stammered out the schoolmaster, cautiously receding from his vehement spouse. "You see now, there! you are excited—very much excited ——"

"Exceedingly excited!" added the lady, with redoubled vigour of expression. "Here I am, from morning till night, working my fingers to the bone for your comfort, Mr. Twiddle. Plating your ruffles—ironing your shirts—darning your stockings—rubbing your great-great-grandfather's nasty shoe-buckles—doing all the plain washing and cooking besides—all for your comfort, for your happiness, sir, and yet I haven't a gown fit to wear. You are a—a—brute, sir," sobbed the indignant wife.

"My beloved Mrs. Twiddle," said her husband, endeavouring to put his arm round her waist, "don't take on so."

"Take away your arm, sir," she vociferated, pushing him away from her with no inconsiderable violence. In doing so, her hand tore open his coat which was buttoned in front, and thus gave to view the two notes which peered out of his waistcoat pocket. "What's that?" she inquired, pointing to them with evident surprise.

"That—my dear," answered the schoolmaster, with embarrassment.

"Yes, sir, that!" said the lady.

"Oh! it's only a few pounds—nothing more, my love—nothing more, I assure you," resumed Timothy, with a smile that plainly denoted how awkward he felt.

"But it isn't all, sir. How did you get it?"

"Ah! you see that's it, my love—that's it. It isn't altogether mine."

"Ours, you mean," interrupted the lady.

"Ours, of course, Mrs. Twiddle; I was going to say so." Here the schoolmaster explained at length to his impatient partner, all the particulars of the mystery, not forgetting to describe minutely any circumstance, however trivial, that was directly or indirectly concerned in the transaction. As he progressed, his eyes, which closely scrutinised the angry countenance of his wife, detected, with infinite satisfaction and delight, the most unequivocal symptoms of returning cheerfulness and good-humour.

"Will I do it, Timmy?" cried the enraptured dame, echoing his last words; "will I do it!—Directly, my love, directly! Mercies! what a windfall! Only think how they'll talk—the Picksniffses, the Chinchillys, the whole village—eh? You'll have a new coat, Mr. Twiddle, and I, a new gown. You'll have a new watch, Mr. Twiddle, and I, a gold chain. We'll go to church together, Mr. Twiddle, and cut the grocer, and the carpenter, and the baker. We'll be aristocratic."

" As our forefathers were before us," sententiously ejaculated Mr. Twiddle, with the unconquerable gravity of a parish beadle at his official inauguration.

After some further congratulations, all of which, however, contemplated the ineffable mortification of the Picksniffses and Chinchillys, Mr. Twiddle leisurely descended the stairs accompanied by his wife, who amused herself by screaming out little Nora's name, until she reached the bottom. The young girl hurried into the house, upon hearing the call, and stood trembling before the lady, who assumed as she entered an air of displeasure and severity, for the probable consequences of which her memory readily supplied the most unhappy analogies.

" Didn't I tell you not to go out this morning ?" commenced the virago. " Oh, you ungrateful little wretch! Don't stand blubbering there — answer me! answer me at once !"

" I didn't hear you, ma'am," said the sensitive child, weeping.

" You didn't, eh ! Well, I've enough of picking up nobody's children ;—get out of my house, you baggage. I give you ten minutes," she continued, pointing to the old rusty clock in the corner, " to pack up your rags and walk ; and then let me never see the sight of you again, you lazy little creature."

" Don't, ma'am, don't turn me out of doors," supplicated the girl. " I wouldn't know where to go—spare me, spare me."

" Out upon you, you vixen !" responded the apparently enraged lady. " Away with you, away !"

With tears that dimmed the lustre of her dark black eyes, the bewildered child proceeded to gather up a bundle of what had the appearance of a few coarse garments, which she secured by means of a thin rope that hung in the closet. While thus engaged, the parrot, from his cage, cried out, " Pretty Nora ! pretty, pretty little black-eyed Nora !" She cast a mournful glance at the bird, and continued her work.

" Now, you may go as soon as you please," said Mrs. Twiddle, observing that she had completed her small package. " What do you stop here for ?"

" Please, ma'am," she said, timidly, " let me tell my geranium good bye ; I know I won't see it again, and it's all that loves me, for I haven't no mother and father, like other little girls have."

" Well, be quick about it, then," croaked Mrs. Twiddle.

Little Nora approached a jessamine tree, standing on the window-sill, whose exuberant greenery and rich white blossoms, almost concealed the disfigured and broken vase in which it grew. After gazing upon it sadly for a moment, she plucked one of the tiny flowers from its stem, which was encircled with a tear, as she transferred it to her bosom.

" Good-bye, mother, sister, brother !" she said, touching, as she spoke, three little branches which crossed each other in the centre ;—her childish fancy, prompted by the yearnings of unspent affection and sympathy, had thus designated them. Turning towards the door, she prepared to depart, when a darkly spotted spaniel jumped from under the cupboard, where it had been slumbering, and frolicked about her path, as if determined to prevent her going. In vain she turned him aside, and repelled his caresses ; he still wagged his tail and barked, and capered about her person.

" Good bye, Sport," she said, trying to force a smile, which only increased her emotion, and caused the tears to flow more copiously. " I can't take you with me, because—you'll —starve."

Thus saying, she turned her red and swollen eyes upon her former protectors, who had mutually refrained from interrupting her, through feelings of remorse and shame.

" Good day, sir—good day, ma'am," she faltered out. " You have turned me away; but God bless you—God bless you !" and bursting into hysteric sobs she took the way which led to a small white paling in front of the house.

Her hand raised the latch, and she paused once more to obtain a last glance of the humble roof which had cradled all her innocent joys and sorrows.

Ting ! sharply echoed a pane of glass in the window, which voluntarily cracked.
Mr. Twiddle started.

" That's bad luck," he said to his wife, shaking his head ominously.

" You're a fool," she replied, sullenly. " What is done is done !"

CHAPTER V.

O, what a goodly outside falsehood hath !—*Merchant of Venice.*

WHEN Rosalind returned to the mansion, after his interview with the schoolmaster, the first question he asked was, whether Blanche had left her chamber during his absence.

This was answered in the affirmative by a prim-looking middle-ged female, whose countenance was rather sour than otherwise, and whom he familiarly designated Lucy.

The words conveying the reply had scarce fallen from her lips when his features assumed a sombre expression, which, however, was only momentary, for he smiled as he observed that her eye rested upon him, and pleasantly remarked, " So much like you, Lucy; you should be more careful."

" I'm getting old," answered the housekeeper abruptly; " my heart and good fortune have been worn out in your service—I can't spare you my eyes."

" You should have an eye to your interest," he mildly observed.

" Coming a long while," ironically returned Lucy.

" Well! well! you are a strange creature, and don't know your friends."

" Don't !" screeched the beldame, dropping her work and staring him full in the face. He affected to look at the flat scenes which the open window discovered to the sight, that he might avoid her piercing gray eyes; and when she resumed her occupation, which took place soon after, cautiously glided from the apartment into his private study.

Here his looks were again gloomy and disturbed, and he hurriedly paced the marble flooring, formed of variegated stone, curiously laid in and shaped after the Mosaic style, whose sharply resounding echoes excited a cold and lonesome sensation in the mind. His dark glances—his irregular walk—his unaccountable gesticulation, all bore the stamp of a mind chased by disappointment, and fevered with accumulating spleen. Now, he nervously seized upon a book from the well-stored shelf—then set it down impatiently, and again paced the chamber with anxiety, still pausing at every turn before a window of stately dimensions, that confronted the lawn. Whatever the evolutions which his singular mood dictated, he invariably returned to this spot, as if expecting to obtain relief from some object, as yet undiscernable, in the barren perspective. But a short time had elapsed, when a man of short stature and singular costume entered the apartment. He wore a faded velvet cap, shaped after the Montero style, and ornamented with a profusion of black ostrich plumes, that partly screened his countenance from observation. His neckcloth which was covered with dust, and slovenly arranged, and his habit generally, which exhibited every indication of reckless abandonment, together with his stern and strongly characteristic features, all conspired to give him the suspicious exterior of a ruffian.

Rosalind started forward upon beholding the stranger, and hastily strode across the chamber to the spot which he occupied.

" Is it done ?" he gasped out with difficulty.

" No," laconically returned the other, shrugging his shoulders with provoking *nonchalance.*

A deep groan, accompanied by a fearful oath, escaped the first speaker, as he struck his clenched fist upon a neighbouring table, with the concentrated energies of madness and despair. Not another syllable fell from his lips ; but bending over the costly furniture which his violent blow had almost destroyed, he looked upon the stranger as if he mistrusted the truth of his intelligence.

" It is so, signor," observed the other, to re-assure him. " By the Holy Mother," he added, " but this matter appears to excite you !"

This was spoken in a dialect which might be Italian or French, but was scarcely recognisable as broken English.

" You're a fool !" cried his enraged host.

" Fool !" echoed the guest, immediately assuming an attitude of defiance, and laying his broad hand upon a rusty rapier, which he wore half unsheathed from its dull leathern scabbard at his side.

" I forgot myself, Marcello," said Rosalind, mending his looks with a gracious smile, and appearing to repent the irreverent expression he had so imprudently employed. " This news comes heavily upon me, and you know me a man of little patience. Forget that ugly word—I did not mean it—I beg of you, forgive me."

" Well, well," answered the stranger, " if you didn't mean it, let it drop here—old friends shouldn't quarrel."

Rosalind had now quite recovered his ordinary composure.

" Pray," he inquired, " how did you miss the little creature?"

" Miss her—Santa Maria ! who wouldn't miss her? Nimble as a deer, cunning as a fox. I chased her a mile, but it was time thrown away. Pooh! she distanced me. Cleared a fence in the twinkling of an eye—scrambled through a hedge—waded a pond like nothing, that I almost got drowned in, following her. My faith on it, signor, she's a weazle."

These incoherent ideas were couched in a singular *melange* of different dialects, which, however, the host seemed to find no difficulty in comprehending.

" And you start to-morrow, you say?" asked the latter.

" Yes, to-morrow—positively. I am obliged to go. Those confounded excisemen are on my track ; they begin to suspect the brigantine."

" This is bad," muttered Rosalind to himself, and he suddenly relapsed into his former thoughtful mood. " Should that hell-cat, Lucy," he vehemently exclaimed, appearing to forget the presence of his guest in the importance of his thoughts, " ever undertake to betray me, she'll have the proof—ay !" he continued, starting up, " the deep—the damning proof of—Signor Marcello, don't mind me—these fits will come on—mere fits— nothing, nothing." His eye had caught that of Marcello, who watched him closely.

" What say you to a glass of Burgundy ?" he cheerfully proposed. The stranger's face signified his perfect acquiescence in the proposal, and Rosalind led the way to a commodious table, on which were tastefully laid out various descriptions of wine, besides other refreshments.

"This to the brigantine," he said, waving his glass courteously, as soon as his rude companion was served. Here the door was slowly opened, and Blanche stood musingly at the threshold, apparently undecided whether to advance or recede. The glass had already reached his lips ere he discovered the maiden, but when he did so, it dropped from his trembling hand, and spilt, as it was crushed to pieces by the fall, its sparkling contents upon the floor.

"Who sent you here?" screamed out Rosalind.

"Lucy told me you had inquired for me," returned the terrified girl.

"Begone!" he peremptorily exclaimed.

"D—n the old hag!" he added, closing the door violently upon the maiden's swiftly receding form.

"I regret that she saw me in this homely garb," remarked Marcello.

"So do I," returned Rosalind. "By-the-bye," he resumed, surveying him with a smile from head to foot, "not such an one as would catch a fair lady's eye."

"It matters little," said the stranger, "that she like my dress or no. Our contract makes me her bridegroom, whatever her whims concerning my person. But—I had almost forgot my errand here; I want funds."

"Funds!" ejaculated the other, astonishment and displeasure both vividly depicted in his louring brow.

"Ay, funds!" repeated the guest. "Is there aught so unfamiliar to your ear in the sound coming from my mouth that you should stare so widely? I say, I want funds."

"Nay, but this is unfair," angrily returned his host. "Have we not agreed? Is there no contract between us? and ——"

"Yes," interrupted the first; "but that is yet to come—*to come!* mark that——it belongs to the future. Hark ye, give me a thousand pounds."

"A thousand pounds!"

"Most certainly—a thousand pounds."

"No?"

"No; are you serious?"

"I'll have you stand to the bargain. Clear me of the little girl and I give you Blanche for wife—two thousand pounds to boot: I'm honest in my dealings!"

"Ah!" said the stranger, with a sneer upon his countenance. "Perhaps you forget," he added, significantly, "the other consideration for this generous agreement. Shall I prompt your memory? and yet, methinks that dismal scene could hardly have escaped it."

"I'll give no more money," cried Rosalind, impatiently.

"Prepare for the consequences, then," firmly answered Marcello, rising abruptly from his seat, and making a few hasty strides towards the door.

"Come now," said his host, in a more subdued tone; "don't be so hasty about it—let us talk the matter over."

"I have no time to waste in words," he responded.

"Will nothing less satisfy you?" inquired the first.

"No! once more, will you give me the money?"

Rosalind did not answer; but, approaching his secretary, reluctantly drew from it a bundle of notes which he placed in the hands of his companion. "There it is," he said, "count them."

"Never mind that," answered the stranger, thrusting the package into a fissure of his colourless vest; "you know better than to deceive me. Farewell! In two weeks I shall return to claim my bride. See that she is prepared to submit. Have you no private passage ?—I must depart."

Rosalind nodded an assent, and without uttering another word led the way. They passed through various apartments, all of which were spacious in their dimensions, and sumptuously decorated. A secret staircase conducted them into a large hall, which opened upon a beautiful garden surrounding the mansion.

They walked, in silence, up a short avenue lined with stately oaks and lofty pines, which terminated in a rough enclosure, more remarkable for its unusual height, than any peculiar gracefulness of design.

"Remember !" said the stranger, solemnly, pausing at the gate, which they had now reached, "in two weeks."

"In two weeks," repeated Rosalind.

A moment more, and the ruffian's form was lost in the dense foliage of the neighbouring forest.

In the meantime, Blanche had retired to her chamber in a state of profound dejection and amazement. The more she pondered over the strange occurrences of the morning, the more her astonishment and melancholy seemed to increase. Her interview with Edward St. Julian—his strange narration, with its fatal oath—his tears at their separation—her innocent intrusion into Rosalind's study—the mysterious stranger, and his darkly-nodding plumes, shading a yet darker countenance—the singular pledge she had overheard, and her father's alarm and anger upon discovering her—all passed in disjointed and incoherent heaps of images before her mind's eye—a wildly-fantastic array of shadowy recollections, which, while it involved her fancy in the bewildering mazes of doubt and terror, signally baffled and perplexed all the resources of analysis.

While thus immersed in various and distracting reflections, her father entered the room. He paused for an instant to contemplate the beautiful being before him; then, adroitly accommodating his features to the emotions he intended to express, bent slightly over her chair, and imprinted a kiss upon her sad and pensive brow, whose matchless lustre neither the cares of disappointment, nor the stings of grief, had the power to obscure. Her arms were immediately stretched out to resist what she mistook for violence; but, on recognising her father, they fell carelessly to her sides, and a bright, though transient beam of satisfaction speedily dissipated the clouds with which her offended modesty had temporarily arrayed itself.

"My dear child," he commenced, "you must deem me harsh and unfeeling to have spoken as I did this morning; but if you knew all I have suffered, and all which I feel it will yet be my lot to endure, you would rather commiserate than condemn your unfortunate father."

"I thought not of it, sir, save with the anxietude to discover in what manner I might have deserved your displeasure," she meekly replied. "Alas! what misfortune has thus suddenly visited you, my father?" added the maiden, in a voice expressive of deep concern.

"One, Blanche, which it is not in my power to avert."

The hypocrite applied a handkerchief which he held in his hand to his tearless eyes, and artfully pretended to weep.

"Nay, my dear father, be comforted," cried the unsuspecting girl, whom this false show of feeling had completely deceived. "Though all the world should leave you, I still

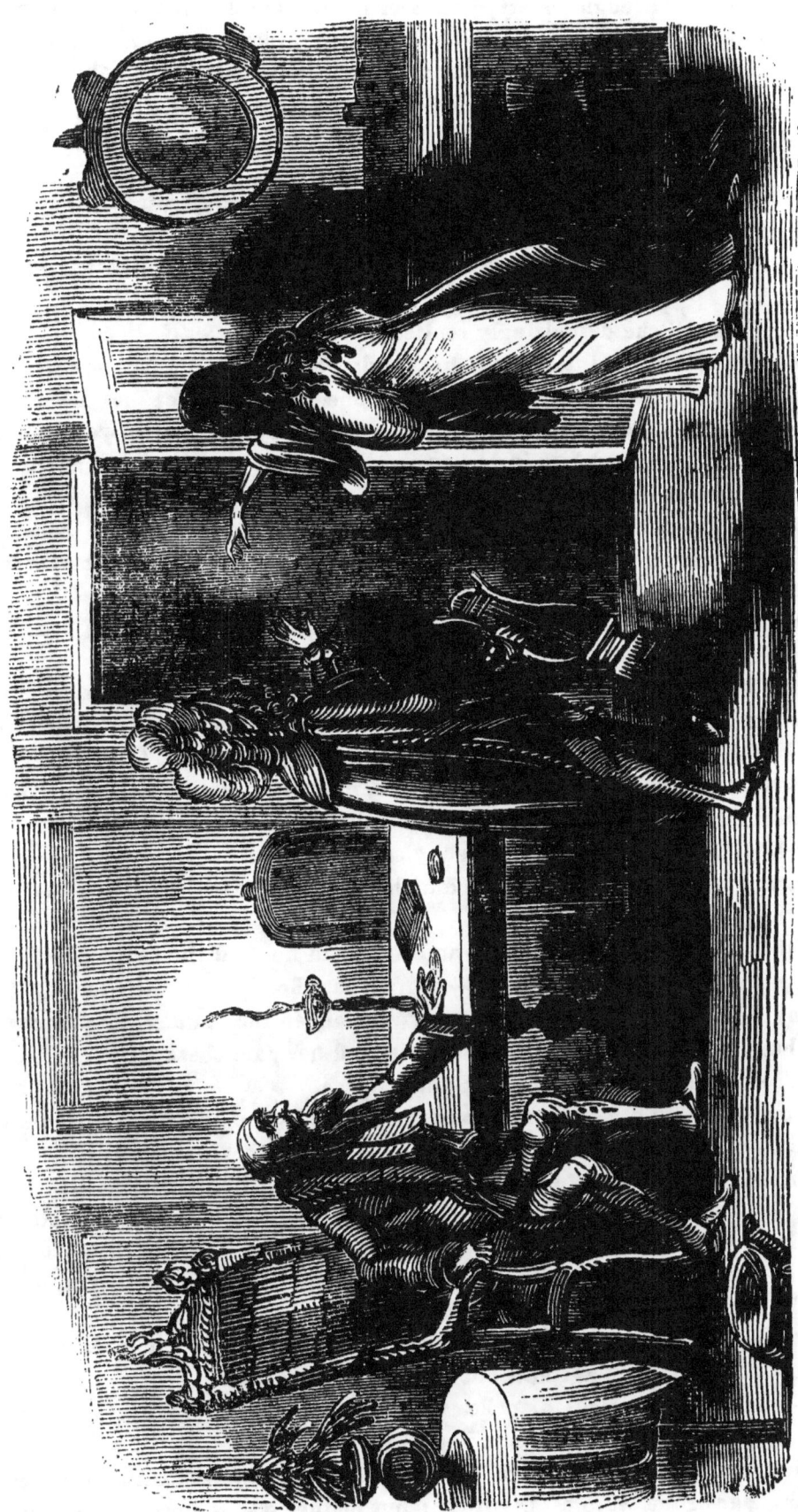

THE STRANGE MASQUE.

[With the noiseless tread of a spirit, the figure glided to the door, and turning upon the agitated youth, waved her hand majestically, as if in token that he was desired to make speed.]

shall cling to your side. Through poverty and scorn, through destitution and despair, will I cheerfully follow your aged footsteps wheresoever they may lead; and while health and life are left me, I can toil and drudge; but your head shall never want a shelter from the storm—no—no," she sobbed aloud, burying her head in his arms.

"Blanche, do not weep, my child," he faltered out. "I doubt thee not—I doubt thee not. Alas! it is not poverty I fear."

"Not the loss of fortune? What else, my father, agitates and depresses your spirits? Speak it to me; if I can do aught; if my life——"

"Not that, Blanche—not that! Thy life! Think'st thou I could accept the sacrifice?"

"Alas! it is all I have," she despairingly replied.

"Listen to me, my child," said Rosalind, uncovering his face, and affecting the most violent emotion; "The misfortune I speak of, is one which cannot be thoroughly explained; seek not to penetrate the mystery. It would destroy a parent in your estimation, for it has already destroyed him in his own. Enough, it is a sin—a damning sin, committed in my youth and inexperience—my days of profligacy and passion. For years I have been reaping its abundant harvest of agonizing and sleepless remorse. And now a fiend stands in my path who would dispute with nature the empty privilege of terminating the worthless life I enjoy. You understand me?"

"I do," firmly replied the maiden, her lips turned to an ashy hue, and her eyes lost in unmeaning vacancy.

"One," he resumed, "whom I thought long since dead, has risen, as it were, from the grave, to blast me. I am his victim—at his mercy—dependent upon him for the charity of breathing. His silence is my *life*—ay, my life. God knows I speak the truth. The gulf of destruction yawns at my feet, and thou alone, my child, can save me from being precipitated into its dismal depths of odium and infamy. I can speak no more. The executioner is ready; let the judge pronounce my sentence."

"I am ready, my father," cries the heroic daughter,—"ready for all things, save to see you die by the hand of——"

Her tongue clove to the roof of her mouth, and she could not end the sentence.

"No, Blanche, I will not. It is a sacrifice—a great sacrifice. I am too exacting."

"Speak it, my father—speak it, I implore you!" exclaimed the maiden, the fervour of filial devotion shining in the spiritual glow that animated her pale cheeks.

Rosalind fixed his eyes earnestly upon her countenance.

"Can you promise to wed other than Edward St. Julian?" he inquired, articulating his words slowly and distinctly.

As the tender sapling is bowed to the earth, and crushed by the fury of the tempest, that young and magnanimous heart fell in speechless agony before the terrible fate that awaited her. Her bosom heaved convulsively, her throbbing temples glistened with chilling drops of perspiration, and tears dimmed her meekly upturned eyes, which seemed to sue for fortitude from a higher and holier Power.

"I see it is too much for you," added the wily parent. "Think no more of it, my dear child, I am old, and have, at most, but few years to live, and——"

"No more!—no more!" cried Blanche, with ghastly composure,—"I am prepared."

He pressed her hand, which was covered with a cold moisture, between both his own, and spoke in language of the warmest gratitude; but neither was the pressure returned, nor the acknowledgments heeded by the maiden. "Farewell! farewell!" she at length broke forth, "my dear, dear Edward. We shall never meet again;" and with these words fell senseless into her cruel father's arms.

"It is done," he darkly muttered to himself, gathering up the prostrate form of the noble girl.

CHAPTER VI.

He was a merry-looking wight,
With visage like the shield of night,
    And curly locks of gray;
Who lov'd all things by nature plann'd,
From Alpine heights to hills of sand,
    And cameos of the clay.

The Naturalist.

AFTER speaking the strange words recorded in a former part of our narrative, little Nora rose from her recumbent position, and issuing from behind the disjointed mass of dilapidated gray stone which had so successfully concealed her from the lovers during their brief interview, stood before Edward St. Julian in all the dazzling sheen of her infantile attractions. He had never before examined her with the scrutinizing minuteness of criticism, and but for the singular language which fell from her lips, would not probably have noticed her more closely on the present occasion. It is true he now dwelt upon her youthful charms with something of ordinary vanity, but its selfish edge was turned aside, and softened by the consciousness of her artless innocence and untainted purity, which, in commending her to his protection, served rather to excite a becoming degree of compassionate solicitude, than to awaken feelings of a warmer nature.

"You are not vexed with me?" said the child, timidly, after waiting a moment for an encouraging word.

"Vexed with you, Nora—no! Why should I be vexed with you?" he inquired, smiling.

"Because I am bad," she answered, looking with embarrassment upon the ground, and blushing deeply.

"Are you?" he playfully exclaimed; "then I am very happy to find you so candid. But tell me, Nora," he continued, in a more serious tone, "how did you find time to come here? Did Mr. Twiddle sanction your coming?"

The little girl ran to her recent hiding-place, and returned with a small packet, whose contents she exposed to his view. Then she hastily recounted the particulars of her sudden discharge from the schoolmaster's employ, and likewise the prolonged and arduous chase a strange-looking man had given her in the forest. While listening to these various details, the young man's countenance alternately indicated the keenest indignation and the deepest surprise.

"Thrust you from the door!" he exclaimed, when she had concluded. "Oh! the ruthless barbarian. Well, well, don't weep, my little girl, don't weep. Accompany me to my father's; he will not refuse you a shelter."

"I am not lazy, sir," said the artless child; "I'll do many things for you. I can run on errands, sweep the house and set the table, and draw water from the big well, near the river."

"Never mind that, my young Venus," answered Edward, and he looked upon her bright face with undiminished pleasure. But few words more were said on either side. Forcing their way through the pigmy trees of tangled copse that terminated in the common road, they had journeyed but a short distance, when a sharp report like that of a rifle rung in their ears. Immediately recovering from the shock, they were preparing to continue in the path, when a good-natured-looking old gentleman, with an empty bird-bag carelessly slung across his shoulders, emerged from the opposite side of the road, and beckoned them to stop.

"Ha! ha! How are ye, Ned? Did you hear that? Egad, I missed it—but saw the feathers—saw them flying in every direction. Narrow escape, boy—very narrow." This was spoken in one breath. "By Jove!" he added, observing Nora, who had lagged behind, and was at first partly screened by the bushes on the way-side, "who is this we have here? Pray, Mr. Ned, what are you doing with this young rose-bud, eh? Tell me that."

The young man briefly related what the young girl had told him, and concluded by mentioning the promise he had made her. During this recital the other did not speak a word; and, when it was over, Edward discovered, upon casting a casual glance at his features, that he was fruitlessly endeavouring to smile away a few tear-drops, that rolled slowly down his cheeks.

"Mr. Merrygold," he said, feelingly, "you are a noble-hearted man; those are honest tears."

"Tears! nonsense, boy. Do you think I'm weeping?" abruptly replied the old gentleman; "not a bit of it, sir; I have never wept since the day I was elected grand secretary of the Royal Entomological and Zoological Society, and that was with joy—hah!"

"Yet, sir, you have no reason to blush for such tears."

"Blush! who told you I was blushing? Odds bodkins! never blushed since Lady Smart told me I looked like an Apollo Belvidere. I was young, then, you dog—cornet in his Majesty's 25th regiment of horse—terrible fellow among the girls. D'ye see, now, I did cry," he abruptly added, "but don't talk about it, you young scamp; and hark ye, Ned, your father is a sedate, melancholy sort of spirit—let me have the little creature."

"Why, Mr, Merrygold, I would willingly ——"

"S'death! none of your whys now. Who says I am not the proper person to take care of the child? Old—nobody to love—nobody that loves me—with an East India bag full, as Jenkins the political economist used to say when I was grand secretary ——"

"Well, grandpa," affectionately interrupted Edward, "we won't disagree; I can refuse you nothing."

"Hist! hist!" exclaimed Mr. Merrygold, pausing suddenly, and placing his hand in front of his young companion—"look at that infant. What a taste! d'ye see—there, there, she's caught the butterfly. Ned, that girl's a paragon. What a glorious member she would have made of the Royal Entomological and Zoological Society!"

Here Nora came running up to her party, whom she had temporarily deserted to secure the beautiful insect that fluttered a prisoner in her tiny fingers.

"Look at it, Mr. Merrygold—Mr. St. Julian," she said, gazing upon her prize with childlike glee; "isn't it handsome—eh? What a heap of shining colours!"

"Ned," gravely observed Mr. Merrygold, "I begin to love that child. She has a turn for natural history. Odds fish! I'll read her the lecture I delivered when I was installed grand secretary of our association—I will—by Jove! I will."

"It is really beautiful," said the young man, admiring it; "what genus does it belong to Mr. Merrygold?" he inquired.

"What genus? Well, I don't know—I should say th—the *Euploea*."

"Why, I thought the different species comprehended in that genus were inhabitants of the eastern continent of Africa," objected Edward.

"So they are!" exclaimed the naturalist. "How did you know that, you dog? Ned, give me your hand—you're a man of taste. S'death! I never met a person that could love butterflies, and the remotest idea of their classifications, that hadn't a soul as big as an Italian cathedral. There now—that's my mind."

"By-the-bye, grandpa," said Edward, whose modesty would not permit him to hear any further comments upon himself, "is it true that you seriously design giving a masked ball, or some other entertainment?"

"Ah! who told you—you rogue? There, d'ye see, I wanted to surprise you all. Faith, what do you think of it, eh?"

"Pleasant diversion," carelessly answered the youth; his mind was constantly recurring to the fatal interview with Blanche.

"Pleasant, Ned—it's glorious diversion!" ejaculated the happy old gentleman. "My birthday, too. I remember when I was grand secretary of the Entomological and Zoological Society, Cornelius Griggs, the poet, said to the Hon. Walsingham Graball, the philosopher—both particular friends of mine—what do you think he said now?"

"Did you say it was to be given on the occasion of your birthday?" asked St. Julian, affecting not to hear the last question, which invariably announced a long story.

"Yes, child," answered the other; "I shall be sixty-three in two weeks."

"Sixty-three, Mr. Merrygold! I would scarce have taken you for sixty."

"Get away, you young scamp," chuckled the sexagenary, with delight, stroking him familiarly on the shoulder. "Ha, ha! sixty, eh? Well, if we hadn't reached the cross-roads, I would tell you a capital old joke about that—Lady Tintel's best. 'Merrygold,' she said to me one day, laughing so sweetly, and showing her ladyship's milk-white teeth—you must know that I was, at that time, grand secretary—hollea!" he exclaimed, suddenly interrupting himself, anxiously looking around, "where's my little girl?—Nora, Nora!"

The maiden had collected in her lap a handful of variously coloured shells, gathered near the margin of the neighbouring river.

"What have you got there, you scapegrace?" cried the good-natured naturalist upon discovering her.

"Such pretty little cups and saucers!" returned the child, with bewitching *naivete.* "Oh! you hear—you hear, they are singing," she added, placing one of the shells to her ear, and listening to its reflected harmonies with girlish joy.

"The fairies live in them, Nora," remarked Edward St. Julian, smiling.

"Do they?" seriously inquired the little girl, wonder and curiosity glowing, in unison, from her darkly beaming eyes. Then minutely examining the gorgeously tinted baubles, which she turned over and over again in her hands, her innocent laugh rang in the ears of her companions like a sudden gush of sylvan melody.

Edward St. Julian turned mechanically from the delighted maiden to his aged friend, who now appeared to scan her features with more than ordinary interest.

"Zounds!" he exclaimed, hastily brushing a tear from his cheek, as if unwilling or ashamed that the other should observe it—"Ned, I've found something."

"Ah!" returned the young man, with an inquisitive glance.

"Egad! the very same smile," he continued, still closely scrutinizing the young girl's countenance. "Odds fish! but they are like two particulars of our species! What a fool I am! never saw it before. Poor Rose Wilton!" and again, despite the most strenuous efforts, his eyes were dim and watery. "'Sdeath! Ned," he abruptly added, "don't look at me so; every heart has its little corner."

"Ned," he resumed, after a slight pause, in a voice husky with agitation and feeling, "I love you, you dog—but I'd fight for that child."

"There will be no occasion for that," answered the young man, smiling, who, having now reached the cross roads, at which they were obliged to part, hastened to apprize little Nora that his promise could not be fulfilled, in consequence of subsequent arrangements concerning her made with their mutual friend. At first, she wept bitterly, but so earnest and touching were the old gentleman's assurances of protection and love, that she finally yielded her consent to their plans with apparent satisfaction.

"Ned," said Mr. Merrygold, briefly, shaking him cordially by the hand, "you've done me a favour, I won't forget it—you can ask for anything—even my bird of Paradise, only one in the country."

"Well, well, we'll reckon the account some other time," pleasantly observed Edward.

"Good bye, Ned; good bye!" said the naturalist. "Don't forget the house—great treat—splendid collection of reptiles—such a lizard! new genus—never known before."

A graceful sweep of the hand, accompanied by a friendly nod, and the young man departed.

"Give me your arm—there, there," cried Mr. Merrygold, passing Nora's arm through his own; "that's comfortable. You're my child, now; remember that. Call me father, I like the name, it makes me feel as if I had really married," he checked himself, adding, mournfully, "poor Rose Wilton; well, you do look her, so you do!"

A hurried pace soon brought them to the dwelling occupied by the benevolent naturalist. It was a plain structure, and though lacking the graceful outline of the Grecian style, and the fantastic ornaments of the Gothic model, there was a cooling freshness and republican simplicity in the modest exterior, which could not fail to charm even the most fastidious taste.

"Here we are!" said the old gentleman, wiping off the copious perspiration from his brow and neck, as they ascended a rude flight of steps which conducted them into the parlour.

"Come along, my little daughter, come along," he said, after they had partaken of some slight refreshments; "I'll show you a world of pretty things, this way."

He led her into a small cabinet, whose tastefully profuse decorations at once announced the peculiar turn of mind which characterized its proprietor. It was lined from top to bottom, on every side, with costly repositories of thick glass, all containing rare and exquisite specimens of natural phenomena. Nora paused to observe a curious collection of entomological rarities, the brilliant hues and felicitous distribution of which enchained her attention and captivated her fancy.

"Are they all sleeping?" she asked, pointing to the butterflies, which occupied no subordinate place in the elegant disposition.

"Sleeping! no, child; they are dead."

"Oh! what a pity," she exclaimed, and her countenance fell at the thought.

"I knew she had a good heart," muttered Mr. Merrygold to himself, shaking his head very significantly at a lion rampant in an opposite case.

That part of the collection to which the child referred was, indeed, well calculated to excite the highest degree of admiration. The objects, which were distributed in happy conformity with the diversities of genera and species, thus pleased the eye by uniformity of arrangement, where they failed to communicate their treasures of instruction to the mind. The cosmopolitan *Pieris,* or white butterfly—the rich and varying yellow of the *Colias* and its sister genus *Cullidregas*—the bright, cerulean blue of the Argus, and the hieroglyphical characters inscribed upon the mystic *Cethosia,* all displayed in their fantastic groupings, where

> "———— on each wing the florid seasons glow,
> Shaded and verged with the celestial bow——"

the gorgeous munificence with which Nature has unsparingly clad the meanest of her subjects.

The little girl turned from the spectacle to survey the other curiosities in which the cabinet abounded. After sating her youthful fancy with their endless varieties, her attention was attracted by a singular shaped panel, ornamented with rich fresco work upon mahogany ground, which formed one of the sides of an alcove or recess terminating in a window that opened upon the south. A delicate touch of the hand, which she passed over its raised flowers by way of examination, sufficed to make it suddenly slide into a secret groove, accompanied by a creaking noise, and thereby revealed to her wondering gaze an oil-coloured representation of a remarkably beautiful female, whose gauzy vestments of cloud, romantic gracefulness, and general ideality of design, gave it rather the appearance of an artistic study than of an ordinary portrait.

" Zounds ! you little ferret, who gave you leave to open that ?" half-humourously inquired the naturalist, being distracted by the strange sound from a grotesque assemblage of insects, which he was examining through a pocket glass, with the all-absorbing interest of a *connoissieur.*

" Is n't she handsome !" cried the delighted child, clasping her hands together and dwelling attentively on the picture.

The sun, which was gradually sinking behind the blazing drapery of the adjacent wood, cast its expiring beams into the chamber, and, by a singularly happy disposition of light and shadows, discovered a striking resemblance between little black-eyed Nora and the mysterious figure of the hidden portrait.

" Jupiter !" exclaimed Mr. Merrygold observing it—" why, she must have been your mother !"

" My mother !" cried the child anxiously rushing up to him—" do tell me, sir, is that beautiful angel my mother?''

" No, my girl,' replied the naturalist lost in astonishment, " don't mind what I say. Great likeness though," he added, looking from the child to the picture. " 'Sdeath ! tremendous likeness !"

" What do you do with that book ?" asked Nora, pointing to a diminutive tome, richly embossed in gold, that lay on an equally diminutive shelf, immediately above the painting.

" That's my prayer-book," seriously answered the old man—" it's time to pray, my daughter. You must learn to kneel down and supplicate the Almighty with your father."

A clock in the adjoining room struck six, and the western sky might now be seen from the window where they knelt together, mournfully sporting its magnificent dyes while struggling to evade the cool embraces of Night's silvery queen, as the fluttering dolphin varies, in death, its evanishing garniture of beauty.

" I'll tell you the story of that picture soon—if you are a good little girl," he said, devoutly joining her tiny hands.

This done she repeated word for word the fervent prayer that fell from his lips, which being over, he raised his downcast eyes to Heaven, and pointed to the evening star which gleamed with spiritual radiance from the faded horizon.

" That's her spirit smiling on us now," he superstitiously observed.

" Don't weep," he continued in half-smothered accents, hastily wiping a tear from his own cheek, and imprinting a kiss upon the girl's—" there, child,—there!—you see I am an old fool—Heaven bless you, you're not fatherless now."

A fresh fountain of feeling was opened in the poor orphan's heart. A strange but gladsome chord vibrated there, and her tears were the refreshing dews of newly awakened joy. The stifled germs of affection had expanded to maturity and blossomed in a fleeting moment:—her sunlight had broken from the cloud. Oh! Nature, who can fathom the depths of thy voiceless sympathies?

CHAPTER VII.

> While words of learned length and thundering sound
> Amazed the gazing rustics ranged around,—
> And still they gazed, and still the wonder grew,
> That one small head could carry all he knew.
>
> GOLDSMITH's *Deserted Village*.

THE time fixed upon by the naturalist for his novel entertainment was rapidly approaching. All the good people of the environs were making diligent preparations to astonish one another on that joyful occasion, by the oddity or elegance of their multiform habits, and the faithful delineation of the personages they were respectively intended to announce. The baker had almost forgotten to supply his customer, so intent was he upon the spangling of a Spanish mantilla which was thought peculiarly appropriate to his costume of Alexander the Great; while the aristocratic Misses Picksniffs and Chinchilly had clubbed together to personate the Graces, in pea-green, scarlet, and hoops. Such being the condition of things, it will scarce afford matter for surprise, that the honest keeper of the Three Black Crows, (a tavern which stood upon the spot now occupied by the Packer's ferry-house, likewise a place of entertainment for man and beast,) was disposed to enlarge, with the onerous loquacity for which his tribe have ever been proverbial, upon the prospects of amusement which the holiday promised.

"Yes, sirs," said he, addressing himself to three of his customers who were seated upon a rude bench opposite to the bar, sipping their liquor, and smoking their pipes, " yes, sirs, there will be great doings here soon! Fun and frolic all round. There's Jenkins —you know Jenkins—glorious fellow, that!—he's got a dress as what will make your mouths run water."

"Tell it us!—oh, out with it!—in course, let's have the character!" simultaneously exclaimed his guests.

"Oh, but that's the secret, you see; can't tell that; out of the question."

"But we are particular friends!" expostulated the three boors.

"Now, sirs, if I only thought I could trust you," resumed the host of the Three Black Crows, with a look that plainly denoted how anxious he was to reveal his budget of intelligence.

"Oh! you can trust me!—and me!—and me!" shouted the company.

"Well, since you will have it, masters—but mind, it's a secret, a great secret, and if you were not particular friends of mine, nobody'd hear it. Remember, *mum's* the word."

TWIDDLE'S ENCOUNTER WITH THE FAIRIES.

[Faster and faster moved the playful measure—faster and faster shuffled the dancer's feet, executing a variety of steps equally remarkable for their ungracefulness and originality.]

All signified their disposition to comply with the condition, and he thus continued,—

"You must know, master, the idea was altogether mine—glorious one, wasn't it?"

"Grand!" ejaculated one of his hearers, as if he already appreciated the felicity of the thought—"Grand!" repeated the other two, who imitated the first, in word and in gesture, very much as a flock of goats follow the steps of their leader.

"Very good," resumed the host. "Jenkins was sitting by the window, and I was talking to his wife—very good sort of woman—you know Jenkins's wife?"

Boors *segundus* looked at boor *primus*—boor *primus* nodded an assent—boors *segundus* did the same.

"Now, what do you think?"

"Think!" presumptuously interrupted one of the subordinates.

"He don't think anything at all—go on," vociferated the prespective organ of the party, glancing fiercely at the subaltern, who had temporarily arrogated a privilege, which he imagined belonged exclusively to himself.

The delinquent quailed beneath the injured eye of the mimic Jupiter.

"Wine! more wine, here!" shouted a loud voice from the back parlour, where a number of young sparks were assembled, who had come from Charleston, to be in readiness for the *fete.*

"Coming, sirs!—coming!" submissively answered the landlord, hastily entering the small enclosure where his wines were arranged in modest but tempting rows, and bustling about with more than ordinary diligence.

"There's that d——d Twiddle!" said the important man, turning towards the door, and curling his lip in supreme contempt at the object of his uncharitable remark, who happened to be passing at the time.

"He's a fool!" added the second.

"A scoundrel!" indignantly observed the third.

"He not only has a bad heart—and you know all about the little girl—a horrid story!"

"Terrific!—abominable!" cried out the others, consecutively.

"But," resumed the first speaker, "he's a man of no pluck; not a bit of it. Would you believe that he is afraid of the Sanctuary?—so he is, my friends! I wouldn't say that word if it wasn't so, if I hadn't the *deerect* proof of the asseveration. Why, he asked me to go with him to Mr. Merrygold, although he hadn't no invitation, merely—mark that now!—merely, I say, to have company when he passes the haunted place. That's it, you see—but I was too sharp for him—ha! ha!— you know me, boys? you know me?"—and he shook his head very significantly, at the thought of his own sagacity and penetration.

"So we do—you're a knowin' un!" chorused his admirers, winking, and shaking their heads, too.

"And, another thing—where did he get so much money from?" inquired the leader, lowering his brows mysteriously, "that's another *pint* of the *argement!* Honest men do not thrive so quickly, masters."

"So they don't," repeated his auditors.

"However, that's no matter of ours," said the speaker, with a motion as of impatience, which, in truth, only meant his desire to force the conversation into a different channel. A moment intervened, and he suddenly resumed—"Mr. Merrygold is an injured man."

The hearers adjusted their pipes, and puffed out such formidable columns of smoke, that their sun-burnt faces were, for a time, invisible to each other.

"I said Mr. Merrygold was an injured man," repeated the leader; "so he is. Sirs, this Twiddle, who is an *ignoramus*, for he actually had the impudence to correct me ——"

"You!" interrupted his companions, astounded at the schoolmaster's presumption.

"Even me, masters!—so he did. Well, I say, this Twiddle of a fellow intends forcing himself as a guest upon a man as what doesn't want his company—who considers him a villain, a deep-dyed, possum-livered villain!" This was accompanied by a variety of gestures with which the speaker sought to strengthen the force of his language, and to impress his sentiments more deeply upon the minds of his hearers. "Again—friends," continued the embryo Demosthenes—"he is going there to eat his dumplins, and tarts, besides other confectionaries—to munch out of the hand what would hit him a d—l of a crack upon the noddle if it only knowed him. Now, what I propose is that we go and diwulgate the secret of his character to the squire."

"Good again! but how'll you know it?" asked his friends.

"Leave me alone," returned the orator with a knowing cast of the eye. "What'll you say, boys, when I tell you I know it already?"

"Wonderful!—extraordinary!" exclaimed the wondering audience.

"Hush!" whispered one of the young sparks in the adjoining chamber to his companions, who had been attentively listening to the above conversation. "Now for the cream of the joke!—more wine, landlord—more wine! D—n him," he added, as the person addressed proceeded to fulfil his commands—"that fellow's itching to go back and narrate his story." All declined their ears with undivided attention.

"Well, I do know it," resumed the man of wit and words; "thus it is, masters. He's going to the masquerade as Junipus Brutus—a celebrated Irishman that was, with Jack boots, made of pasteboard."

Here a deafening roar of laughter burst from the next apartment, that had the effect of rendering the trio more circumspect as to the colloquial pitch of their voices, which presently subsided into an almost inaudible whisper.

"This is glorious," cried the young man before alluded to, abruptly closing the door of the chamber in which his party were assembled, so that the boors should hear nothing of the merry freak which he intended proposing to his friends. "Fair opportunity," he continued, after having concluded the operation; "fair opportunity for a lark, gentlemen, at this clown's expense. What, if we should personate the goblins, grim and ghastly, of this haunted Sanctuary, and frighten the Roman patriot out of his senses?"

"Ha! ha! ha!" laughed the company, who were unanimously pleased with the felicitous suggestion.

"Bottlegreen is a poet," resumed the speaker, tapping a gaily dressed individual, to his left, upon the shoulder; "he'll prepare our parts. Let me see—three, six, eight! By St. George, there are enough of us to scare a whole regiment of infantry upon a nocturnal expedition. You consent, gentlemen, of course?"

"Certainly! certainly!" shouted his friends with one voice.

"Now, boys," he continued, with mock gravity, "having constituted ourselves ghost in chief of this party of grave-haunting and little boy-eating band of supernatural nightwalkers, we do hereby, with all necessary solemnities, ordain, commission, and appoint Emmerson Smith and Bottlegreen, our bard, spirits of note and distinction. The others we make fairies extraordinary in consideration of their being present:—the common witches we shall import from Charleston per first available opportunity.

These quaint observations were repeatedly interrupted by the inexpressible mirth of his companions, who were more than delighted with the pleasantry his humourous fancy had devised.

"Here's to the health of *Generalissimo* John Hasleton," cried Bottlegreen, the poet, raising his glass to his lips, "commander-in-chief, and most paternal potentate of the spiritual forces of the Ashley, and his devoted victim, Junius Brutus Twiddle."

"Standing, boys, standing!" exclaimed a gentleman, in sky blue small clothes and silver buttons.

"Standing, boys!" sung out all the merry-andrews, at once.

"That won't do, Bob—fill up your glass, or we'll salt you," familiarly thundered one.

"Those are my sentiments! salt that white man. Yahou! hou—hou!—Yahou!" sharply whooped a comical looking student, whose quizzical leer and childish hilarity plainly indicated his superlative contempt for the brood of temperance and moderation.

"Now for it," resumed the toaster, lifting outright his glass, with each pealing cheer that rang through the diminutive apartment. "Hip, hip, hurra!!" and with one unanimous accord, the party drained, at a draught, the sparkling contents of their foaming goblets.

———

CHAPTER VIII.

You know, since Pentecost the sum is due,
And since I have not much importun'd you;
    *   *   *   *
Therefore make present satisfaction.   *Comedy of Errors.*

THE two weeks which Marcello had appointed for the consummation of his contract with Rosalind, were fast drawing to a close; one day only remained, and that had nearly expired. It was dusk, and the flitting shadows of twilight stole, with darkling footprints, over weed-grown hillock and blasted heath. Field and meadow were rapidly losing their sprightly adornments of light and shade, and already the west wind was chanting its evening psalm to mazy rivulet and muttering stream. With prolonged and piercing shrieks, the cranes sought their marshy coverts in each boggy moor, and the beetle's dreamy hum, now and then broken by the cricket's monotonous note, welcomed, in advance, the starlit season of solitude and repose. A rosy beam yet lingered on the swiftly rolling waves of the Ashley, when a suspicious looking personage, who had probably been travelling along its borders, might be seen diverging from his tract in the direction of the road which led to Rosalind Mansion. His vestments, which were somewhat soiled by the dust, were of a sombre gray, and their style of make thoroughly English. His hat was sunk deeply over his brow, and thus rendered less recognizable to the glance of passing observation a countenance which it could not effectually conceal from its more careful scrutiny. But, notwithstanding this artful disguise, it was easy enough to discover in the stranger our old friend Marcello, now divested of his notable appendage of cap and feathers, doublet and hose, and clad in a garb, which had the double advantage of being more pleasing to the taste, and inviting to the eye. With hasty strides he advanced through the forest, and speedily reached the main road. Here he frequently glanced around him with anxiety, as if apprehensive of detection, and still increased his pace with each manifestation of alarm, until his walk bordered upon a degree of speed which is usually designated by a more appropriate appellation.

"Here I am!" he exclaimed, in his peculiar medley of tongues, upon reaching the lawn in front of his coadjutor's study. "By the beard of St. Julian—if the holy father had one—I have had a walk for a feast." Saying these words, he gave a shrill whistle, which was answered by the appearance of Rosalind's head at the casement, who beckoned him to betake himself immediately to an apartment on the lower floor, where a secret flight of stairs gave access to his own. But though this was accomplished with a celerity of comprehension and movement that did infinite credit both to him that gave the order and to him that executed it, the latter's person had not escaped the sleepless vigilance of another eye. From her seat in the dining-room, Lucy had watched the Italian with a mistrustful look; and when, upon following her master's directions, he suddenly disappeared, she hastened to his study, and gliding softly behind a massive screen, covered with ancient figures and devices, which accidentally confronted the door, prepared to make the best of the advantage which it gave her.

"You are punctual," cried Rosalind, shaking the ruffian's hand coldly, as he entered. "Somewhat before your time, for the sun is scarcely set."

"Better early than too late, is my rule in matters of this kind," abruptly answered the Italian, who was hurt at so indifferent a reception from his companion. "How is it with the girl?"

"So—so—master, quickly to business. Honest gentry begin with civilities," sarcastically observed his host.

"Honest gentry!—civilities!—humph!—we can dispense with that," muttered the other doggedly, disposing of his hat and throwing himself upon a chair. "Are you dumb," he continued, "or do you intend answering my question? Is the girl quite willing?"

"She is," laconically replied Rosalind.

"So much the better for you, signor—so much the better for you. I would grieve that you should lose your precious neck. By the keys of St. Peter, methinks it is more pleasant to have it encircled by a harmless Barcelona, than the hangman's knot."

"I see you are disposed to rail, Marcello," coolly answered his host.

"So I am, so I am, signor, and yet precious poor spirits to rail withal. The pains of fatigue in my limbs, and the thoughts of a cursed woman in my brain; these are troublesome companions, you'll own."

"A woman!" exclaimed Rosalind. "What mean you?"

"Oh, nothing but a little demoiselle, signor, that I have kept about the vessel to keep off the Evil One's curse. I met her in Florence, and made bold to ease her mother of the fair burden; so she has followed me since, and begins to think now that she has as much right to my person as if the Holy Church, instead of the black spirit, had tied our knot."

"Ah!" thoughtfully muttered Rosalind, in whose mind the prospect of an obstruction to the schemes he had concocted with the Italian excited a secret delight.

"So it is; but, by the Holy Mother, I'm not to be trifled with—she shall find it so," continued the speaker, with a vehemence of utterance that seldom appeared in his speech, which, though plain and rough at times, was habitually mixed up with no inconsiderable portion of the mildness and suavity so characteristic of his nation.

"Does she suspect your intention?" eagerly inquired his crafty companion.

"Ay, she suspects. What of that? The d—l can't bless himself with holy water more awkwardly than I can tell the truth, so I was e'en in my element, you observe; and, being as much afraid of her tongue as you are of mine, signor, I told her a fine story, which the fool suspects and believes, believes and suspects by turns; a kind of uncertainty very much like that of the thief whom St. Swithin of blessed memory proved so, by making the sheep he had stolen bleat in his pudding, for he couldn't say one thing or another, which is the case with *La pauvea figlia*, that I left, in this condition, for Florida, which I have reached, as you see, signor," continued the ruffian, smiling.

"But do you not fear detection?"

"Fear! Signor Rosalind—fear! that's a word for cowards. I fear nothing. However, let us discourse no further of such trifles—are you ready to fulfil your promise? To-morrow, you know, is the time, which I will extend to three days more, that you may say your pater and be prepared. I'm not ill-natured, you see."

"Thank you, Marcello," said Rosalind, with unaffected delight; "this is generous of you, indeed—I did not——"

"Expect it," added the Italian. "Well, well, signor, I forgive you—this is no season for compliments. And, besides, what care I for them? My calling requires them not, and therefore have I none of your vile tricks of insincerity and deception in my nature. I am for north or south, east or west—just to the point—with only one compass. No double meaning—no backsliding—no stabbing in the dark. If I pilfer you, you have the satisfaction of seeing the artist; that's professional, you see, signor; but then, there are so many picaroon thieves who disgrace our noble craft, and sink it into a matter of mere pewter and pins, that I am almost loth to pursue it. By the holy rood, I would that those interlopers were burnt for incense, though I'm certain it wouldn't ascend to Heaven if they were the material."

While Marcello spoke, a smile of complacent satisfaction played around his lips, and gave them an expression of good-humour, which, in some measure, contributed to soften the habitual harshness of his features. Rosalind's manner during his discourse was, indeed, that of the most undivided attention, but a certain vagueness of glance commonly indicative of mental abstraction, did not fail to convince the speaker that his witticisms were both unheeded and unappreciated. This, joined to the fatigue he had undergone, persuaded him to end an interview, in which his conceit saw so little probability of gratifying, or being gratified itself.

"Well, signor," he said, after waiting a few moments for a reply from the other, "are you going to doze? To judge from your serious looks, one would think you are travelling over a penance of six months—and that meted out by the pious order of St. Bernard."

"No—no," said Rosalind, awaking somewhat suddenly from his profound reverie; "pray—forgive me, Marcello. I have had some matters of moment preying upon my spirits:—I beg of you—regard it not. By my troth, now I come to look at thee, thou hast been sadly neglected by thy churl of a host. You want refreshment and sleep more than talk and cheerfulness, methinks. Follow me; I can afford you both—we won't stand upon ceremony—up, man, up, you are lazy—come!"

With these words they were preparing to leave the chamber, when a slight noise, as the rustling of a female garment, assailed their ears.

"Stop! did you hear nothing?" inquired the master of the mansion, pausing, and inclining his head attentively.

"No," answered his drowsy companion, yawning and rubbing his half-closed eyelids—"the winds, signor. I presume—only the wind."

"Well—perhaps so, or probably my fancy," continued Rosalind; "but still 'tis strange; methought I heard something behind that screen." So saying, he left the study, followed by the Italian, who was muttering incoherently to himself some of those vague and disconnected ideas which usually prevail between waking and repose.

While these circumstances were transpiring, an event took place at the Three Black Crows which puzzled and perplexed its keeper's wits in no ordinary degree.

An awkward and unattended female presented herself at the bar, at a time when that public apartment, luckily for her *incognito* happened to be perfectly empty. This purely accidental circumstance, however, was regarded by the sagacious host with no common feelings of suspicion, and occasioned him to propound several questions to the stranger which were rather more remarkable for impertinence than courtesy. She overlooked them all, briefly stating her intention of remaining a short time in the village, and likewise a wish that the matter should be kept still and secret: a piece of intelligence, which, inasmuch as it was accompanied by the tender of a glittering though unfamiliar coin, at once subdued all the innkeeper's ideas of propriety, and convinced him, beyond a doubt, that she was a very decent sort of person.

The stranger's countenance was of that peculiar cast, which betrays exquisite symmetry of feature unallied to those softer traits and more captivating graces of expression, that make up the character of true loveliness, in her sex. But, though one might admire her beauty without danger, it was impossible to dwell upon it without awe. There was an indescribable air of softness and superiority in every word and gesture, which the beholder simultaneously acknowledged, and disposed himself to obey. The credentials of sway appeared naturally woven in the snowy texture of her commanding brow, and her tall, queen-like form, and corresponding majesty of demeanour, rendered her a much fitter representative of the stately goddess of Olympus than the faithless divinity of Paphas.

"Jest please to follow me, ma'am," said the querulous owner of the Three Black Crows, upon receiving the gold; "I'll show you the best room in the house. There's only four, any how; and may be you'd like to have your choice; but three of them is occupied—all by respectable people, though, I'll warrant you, ma'am. There's Hobbs, the smith, and Mistriss Mink, the milliner, and Quirk, the tinker. Talking of Quirk, ma'am, you may have hern about his children; but they don't make as much noise as they used to did. Dark passage this; but you'll soon get to the room, ma'am. Elegant bedstead and chairs, besides a looking-glass, tall as the ceiling, and a guitar, with only one string missin'. Oh! I was just going to forget the backgammon-box,—you plays on backgammon, I suppose, ma'am?"

The lady shook her head in reply, but did not speak.

"Talking of backgammon," continued the speaker, "I seed a chap this afternoon as what made a fool of me on that same game two weeks ago. 'Landlord,' says he, 'let's play a game.'—'Mister,' says I, 'I doesn't play.' Well, he parleyed about it, and, finally, somehow, we did play, and I got stuck. All right, though, ma'am,—all right! That'll jest teach me how to play with outlandish fellows again, as what wears feathers in their hats."

"What did you say?" inquired the stranger, with surprise. "A man that wore feathers in his hat?"

"Yes, ma'am, jest so; the biggest sort of them you ever did see. I saw him cutting to Mr. Rosalind's house fast as he could, with bran new clothes on; but I knowed him for all that; so, says I, 'Halloo, you sir! jest wait a minit.'"

"Of course, you received no answer," observed the stranger.

"Nothin', ma'am; you are right there agen. He was as deaf as a jug."

Having reached the chamber, the talkative host paused as if disposed to continue the colloquy which his new guest had so patiently endured on their way to it; but a slight inclination of the hand sufficed to dismiss him from her presence, an operation which he did not fail to accompany with a very low obeisance.

"So,—so," she whispered, slowly closing the door, and throwing herself upon a chair,

" to Florida is it that you have gone, Signor Marcello?   Let them trample on the worm who fear not its sting; 'tis sometimes deadly—deadly—deadly."

Dropping her dark eyes upon the ground, which, as she repeated these words, darted forth a gleam of apparent defiance and triumph, she was speedily immersed in a train of reflections which invested her matchless features with the alternate mutations of despondency and passion.

CHAPTER IX.

Philosophy is a bully that talks very loud when the danger is at a distance; but the moment she is hard pressed by the enemy, she is not to be found at her post, but leaves the brunt of the battle to be borne by her humbler, but steadier comrade, Religion, whom, on all other occasions, she affects to despise.—Lacon.

WE return, in the natural course of our desultory narrative, to the elder St. Julian. Worn out by the weight of premature decrepitude, and tormented with its concomitant infirmities, he was daily advancing with feebler step to his grave, which, with the blissful credulity of the human mind, he still fondly trusted would not, at once, extinguish his memory and his name.   True, the fatal prophecy was fulfilled but in part, which was to stamp, in dreariness and desolation, the vengeance of an injured sire upon the deserted hearthstone of his exterminated race.   But Hope, the beautiful delusion of the heart, ever glided into his darkest forebodings, and dissipated the shades of melanlancholy with her sunl ght and her smiles.   The goddess revealed herself in all her tinsel and pageantry to his bewildered sight, and, deluded by her arts, he stretched wide his arms to clasp a fleeting cloud to his bosom.   Yet it was comfort to the comfortless wretch to be deceived, who had nothing to expect from man or to entreat from fortune.   " Repentance and forgiveness—penitence and pardon!" whispered the siren's voice; and, childlike, he listened and believed.   The malediction, like a tempest which temporarily devastates and darkens, would soon vanish from the horizon, which it only disturbed to purify; his ardent supplications were granted above, and his child, at least, would escape the dreadful doom, which, conscious of deserving himself, he shrank not appalled from encountering.

Though this serious disposition of mind had declared itself only since his recent interview with Edward, its happy effects were already distinctly observable in his demeanour and actions.   The proud head no longer satirised the bleeding heart, but was bowed down with becoming meekness and resignation.   The wild and haggard glances of impatient suffering seldom distorted the placidity of his features now, in whose unaffected mildness the finger-traces of angel spirits might be discerned.   The furrows of care were indeed visible still, yet they were such as betoken a refined and exalted sorrow, and not the fitful start and vacant stare of ungovernable frenzy.   The groundless speculations in which he once effectually sought to drown the tortures of reflection and memory, were deservedly laid aside and despised, while the fountains of revelation were invited to flow through the channels which they had occupied, and to pour their healing waters upon his scared and broken spirit.   And even when the gratuitous consolations of hope failed him, and a painful conviction of his unavoidable destiny flashed across his mind, he murmured not, as of yore, but summoned all the Christian's fortitude to meet the Christian's fate.

The day fixed upon for the celebration of the long expected festival had, at length, arrived.   Evening was walking the skies with her silver targe and jewelled host, whose

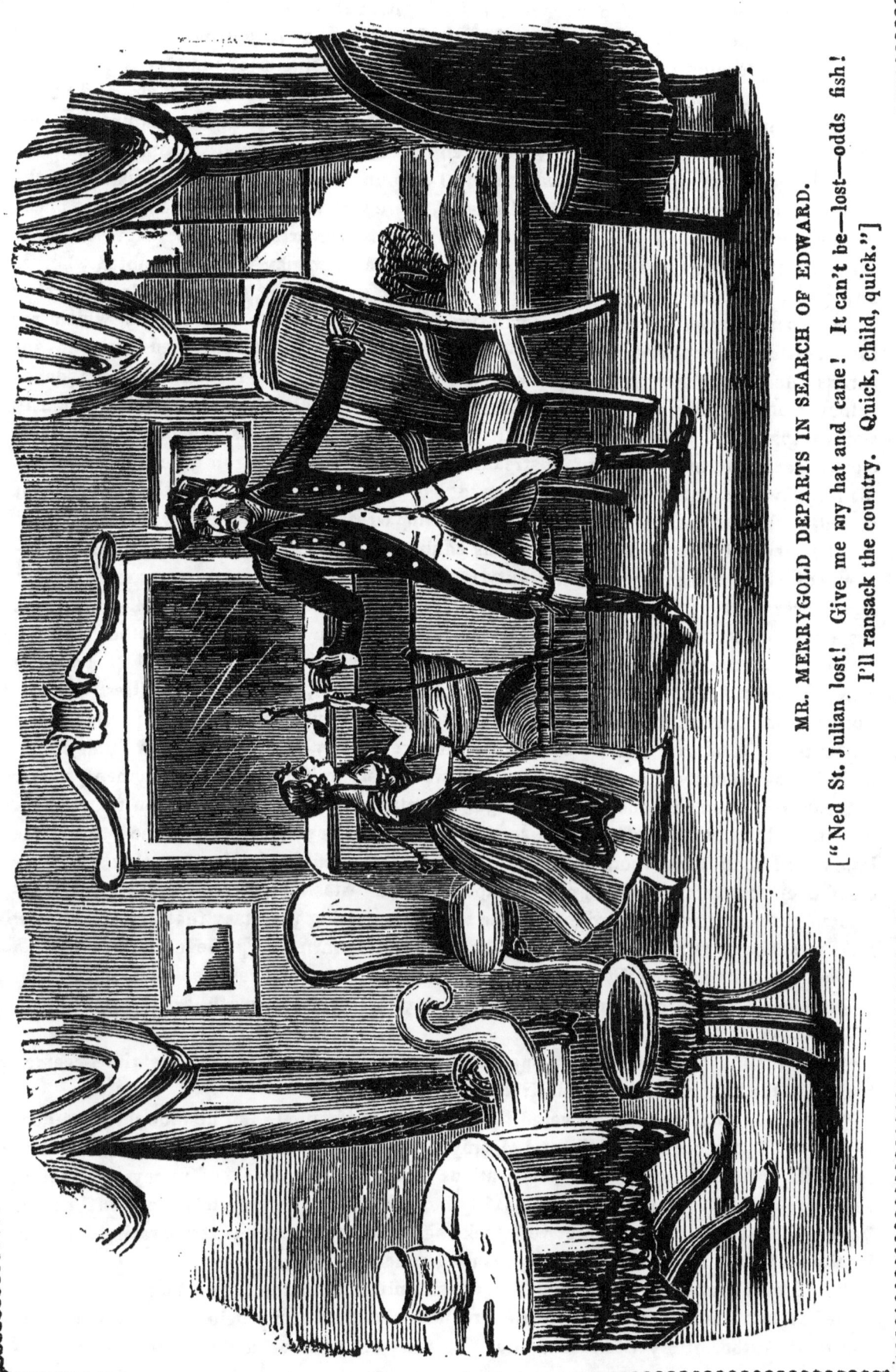

MR. MERRYGOLD DEPARTS IN SEARCH OF EDWARD.

["Ned St. Julian, lost! Give me my hat and cane! It can't be—lost—odds fish! I'll ransack the country. Quick, child, quick."]

mild lustre, here and there darkened by the fugitive shadows of the landscape, was now and then startled by the fitful glare of the reveller's torch, as he journeyed to the scene of revelry. According to custom, the old man was seated in his chamber. A ponderous family bible lay open before him, dimly illuminated by a neighbouring lamp, and beside the table on which it rested, stood his son. But though the changeful posture, and impatient looks of the latter, plainly indicated his desire to terminate a conference which had not yet commenced, and it was natural enough to suppose him anxious to join the happy party assembled at Merrygold Mansion, there was another attraction in that place, which far transcended this last in his judgment. Nevertheless, his disguise rather favoured the former presumption than otherwise, and it may well be doubted whether any one would have conjectured from its brilliant decorations, that his object in going thither soared beyond the ordinary vanities of youthful folly. His costume, which was intended to represent one of the genteel brotherhood of Song that flourished in the adventurous times of Chivalry, was uncommonly tasty and elegant. It consisted of a dove-coloured doublet, and trunks of similar material and dye, thickly studded with variously stained glass, and jewellery that sparkled with dazzling brightness. A purple mantle or cloak, deeply laid in with alternate streaks of silver and gold, hung in graceful folds about his form, which, with a richly embroidered hat, surmounted by a frail white plume that curled, with each passing breath, as a quivering wreath of snow, and was secured by a small aigrette of diamonds, completed his equipment; the general disposition and ornaments of which, were more in conformity with the suggestions of a gorgeous taste, than a rigid observance of historical proprieties. To these might be added a well-tuned lyre, suspended by a modest band around his neck, which in announcing, together with the rest of his attire, the modern character he personified, in no wise tended to lessen a striking resemblance which, at first sight, revealed itself, between his faultless proportions and the ornamental paintings and statues of the Deity that anciently presided over his assumed calling. The old man raised his eyes slowly from the sacred volume which he had been attentively perusing, and after dwelling upon him sadly, for a moment, spoke.

"Edward," he commenced, "a strange presentiment has taken possession of my soul. You may deem it chimerical, but a secret voice, even now, whispers to me—this is the last time I shall look upon you. Nearer, nearer, my child; forgive me that I throw a cloud over your merry mood, and, perhaps, create a distaste for the enjoyments you anticipate. I know you will pronounce it a whim—a passing phantasy that age and sorrow have wrought up to alarm me. Ah! believe it not—I warn you, believe it not! Till a moment past, I yet ardently hoped that the prophecy should be revoked; but lights from another world have broken upon my vision. My hour has, at length, arrived. Edward, I shall never see thee more!"

A spiritual lustre shone in the speaker's eyes, and his cheeks, for the time, seemed bathed in the hallowed light of inspiration.

"Alas! my poor father," answered the youth, more terrified than he thought it prudent to exhibit, "your constant vigils and gloomy thoughts have waked this appalling phantom into life. Mind it not. The dispensations of Heaven are those of mercy, and not of revenge; and a penitent sinner may safely hope for pardon, since its benevolent decree declares that the weary wanderer who seeks again the paths he has temporarily deserted, by that act itself atones for the unrighteous dereliction."

"And have I not felt its mercy?" eagerly inquired his father; "I who for years murmured and upbraided—cursed my fate—reviled the laws of my being, and thus insulted the great Author of my destinies; and this, too—all this, at the very threshold of the

Asylum which he offers, as a refuge, to the penitent criminal. Have I not been heard? have I not been answered? have I not been strengthened and consoled? Thus much has the crushing Atlas that pressed the worm to his native earth been eased by the hand he scoffed at, in his impious littleness and pride. But what is writ is writ, and cannot be effaced. The tomb has sent forth its witness against the parricide," continued the speaker, rising from his seat, and clinging tremulously to the table for support; "retribution has set its seal of condemnation—blood was the forfeit, and blood shall the atonement be! I ask no more; I would not add sacrilege to my sins."

These last words were smothered in his throat, as he paused, his eyes rivetted upon the youth, who quailed beneath their supernatural glances, and vainly attempted to collect himself and speak.

"You have heard it, my son," he resumed; "it is no whim of thought, no distempered vision. Ay, thou may'st weep, my dear boy; I, too, could play the child, but that the fountain is drained of its refreshing moisture now. Look thy last—for last it is, upon the poor old man who tells thee this; and shouldst thou survive his fall, and one day in sorrow linger at his grave, bethink thee that its cold and speechless inmate loved thee better than his life; but that his manifold afflictions are over, and that he smiles in peace upon thee from on high. Farewell! I shall soon meet thy mother in a better world. There, my son, God be with thee, now and evermore."

Edward St. Julian wept violently upon receiving his father's blessing, and what the latter declared, in a voice whose prophetic mission could not be mistaken, to be his last embrace. Again and again he kissed his wrinkled cheeks, and sobbed aloud to think the old man should be deserted and alone, in the fatal hour of earthly dissolution. While these melancholy reflections coursed each other with dizzy fleetness through his brain, he knelt in silence at the doomed one's feet, and, with arms clasped around his neck, ever and anon pressed him more closely to his throbbing breast. It was a scene too full of melting pathos and reachless sublimity for the hand of genuine art to embody with fidelity; and a Raphael, warmed by the tender sympathies of exalted genius, would have dropped his pencil in the fruitless attempt, in order to commiserate the humble and contrite father, or to weep with the afflicted son.

The former first broke the painful silence which ensued.

"My dear child," he said, "I know you design to test the truth of what I have said, by endeavouring to oppose any circumstance that may apparently have the lamentable tendency of verifying my prediction; but, remember, when you do so, that you act not only in opposition to the will of God, but that of your father also, who is prepared to meet his fate, and would not have it retarded."

"Your injunction shall be obeyed strictly," answered the young man, striving to regain his composure. "Since you deem it the decree of a higher power, it were an idiot's thought to seek to resist the Being whom I adore. I repeat it, you shall be obeyed."

"There is one thing more, Edward," resumed the old man, "that I would speak of ere we part. It has weighed heavily on my mind, and often occasioned me to think, while I implored the clemency of God, that the mercy would be refused me which I had denied unto another. I mean," he continued, "the oath that I sinfully pressed upon your conscience, in a moment when my darker passions were aroused."

"And is it not still obligatory?" inquired Edward with surprise.

"I have forgiven," said his father, evading the question, "and with my last breath shall forgive, Philip Rosalind, and—"

Here the servant entered the chamber in breathless haste, saying that a strange woman demanded an interview immediately with Edward St. Julian, and was, even then, at the door, where she had followed him, despite his entreaties and exertions to prevent it.

"Shew her in!" said the father.

The order had scarce been given, when a mysterious apparition of a female, clad in flowing robes of pure white, with locks of raven darkness falling in Bacchanalian profusion and disorder down to her ungirdled zone, stood forth in the centre of the apartment. With one hand she slowly beckoned the servant to retire, while the other was employed in securing beneath her chin the folds of a thick black veil, which, being so adjusted that it effectually screened her features from observation, seemed intended to excite curiosity with a promise of baffling its inquiries.

"A masker, I presume," suggested the old man, whose recent habits of thought and gloomy presentiments barely left room for astonishment at a sight so well calculated to alarm any other mind.

"Ay," answered the figure, promptly, "but on no masker's errand." Turning to Edward, she added, "I sought thee. If thou wouldst save from destruction what most thou lovest on earth, tarry not, but follow me!"

Startled by these strange words and the yet stranger being who had uttered them, the young man would have shrunk in amazement and terror from complying with her request; but a gleam of that rapid perception which often visits bewilderment of mind designated his father as the probable object of her ambiguous warning, and, stepping forward, he said, in a subdued but firm voice, "Go on—I attend you!"

With the noiseless tread of a spirit, the figure glided to the door, and turning upon the agitated youth, waved her hand majestically as if in token that he was desired to make speed.

"Farewell, my dear father," he said, embracing him, "once more, farewell."

"For ever!" concluded the old man solemnly, gasping for breath as he strained the boy to his bursting heart.

Again the stately figure waved her hand, impatient of his delay.

The youth observed it, and releasing himself with one effort from his parent's arms, proceeded to do her bidding. All the awful composure of settled distress appeared in the latter's countenance, as he dwelt, in agony, on the receding form of his beloved child. A few seconds, and the figure had reached a turn in the long and dimly lighted corridor which led into the chamber. Like a shadow, fainter and fainter, she approached it—like a shadow she flitted past. Treading fast upon her footsteps followed his son. A long breath—an eager inclination of the hand—a sudden start, and the object of his fondest affections was lost to his sight for ever.

The old man's knees gave way, and he fell in the prostrate attitude of supplication. A momentary struggle ensued between parental grief and Christian fortitude; but the latter finally prevailed, and with the humility of a truly penitent mind, strengthened by its internal consciousness of rectitude and favour, he clasped his withered hands together, and fervently exclaimed, "Father of Nature! thy will be done on earth as it is in Heaven."

CHAPTER X.

Fal.: I do begin to perceive that I am made an ass.
Ford: Ay, and an ox, too ; both the proofs are extant.
Fal.: And these are not fairies ?   I was three or four times in the thought they were not fairies ; and yet the guiltiness of my mind, the sudden surprise of my powers, drove the grossness of the foppery into a received belief, and in spite of the truth of all rhyme and reason, that they were fairies.   See you, how evil may be made a Jack-a sent, when 'tis upon ill employment.
Merry Wives of Windsor.

We take leave for the present of the mysterious female and her bewildered attendant, who are threading their way through the moonlit forest, and direct our attention to the band of merry-andrews from Charleston, diligently employed, during this time, in accomplishing the mischievous project they had devised.

Appareled in long robes of white linen, fantastically ornamented, and armed with broomsticks and wands, they hastened to take the stations respectively assigned them by their leader, in the thick and tangled shrubbery that enclosed the wizard spot.

"All ready now," cried Hazleton, whose tinselled head-dress and other conspicuous marks of distinction announced his superiority over the rest, after he had disposed his gay companions in proper order ; "prepare for the signal ; as soon as it's given, go to work.   You all know your parts, boys."

"Yes, yes !" answered bush, ruin, and tree, at once.

"Tomkins," resumed the first speaker, addressing himself to the comical student, "I half suspect you have forgotten your part ; that last drink did your business."

"Hasl-l-ton," stammered this individual, clinging more closely to a sturdy oak that concealed him, for the support denied by his legs ; "I con-sid-er-r you as a-a shabby whit-t-te man !   I have-obser-ved with the ut-most pain, that you mean t-t-to dete-rio-rate from the charac-ter of a gentle—hic !—of a gentle—hiccup !—of a gentle-e-man : d'ye hear ?"

"Silence !" shouted several voices.

"I wo-wo-won't be silent.   I stand up—hiccup !"—here one arm gave way, and he almost lost his equilibrium—" in the vindication of my priv-leges—im-m-m-unit-ies—and rights !"

"Oh, you are drunk !" again interrupted the others.

"I un-e-e-quiv-cly de.y that—hic !—that sland-rous as-pe-pe-persion !   D—n these trees ! how they're dancin-up a-a-and down.   Gentlemen—dud—dud—don't consid-er that I'm at all in-e-briate.   I'm perfectly so-so-sober.   He ! he !   Bottlegreen—you're tree's going to—fall down.   There it goes ! — Yahou — Yahou-hou-hou—Yahou !— deu-u-ce take me o-f-ff.   I'll be a-a-an ordin-ary witch."

"Oh, stop, stop ; you'll spoil that fun," remonstrated his companions.

"I dud — dud — don't care — hiccup !   I'm a free and inde-pendent ci-i-it-zen. When in th-h-e course of—human ev'nts it be-be-becomes nes-ary—hic ! for one nation to dissolve the po-po-po-litical bands that—unite them—to another, a white man ought-ent to be—a—witch.   Fellows !   I want to make a speech—I'll make a speech now—hold on ! he ! he ! look at all the trees—playing pussey in a corner."

Here Hasleton, expecting the subject of their joke at every moment, was obliged to interpose, and with threats, entreaties, supplications, finally succeeded in silencing the obstrepulous fairy.

"I understand yo-u to apol-gise, Hasleton," said the student.

"Certainly—certainly."

"Well—that'll do. Look here—though—do-don't consi-der that I'm drunk."

"Of course—of course. Be still, man, confound it! you'll mar the sport.",

"I'll b-e-e still—-then—I'm sober as—a judge. Just let go my arm! Do-do-don't shake this tre-tre-tree—I—I—knew it was somebody." After this brief colloquy the leader resumed his former position, and prepared to receive the expected guest with all the hospitalities of witchcraft.

In blissful ignorance of the fate that awaited him, Mr. Twiddle busied himself in arranging the various parts of his disguise, and, at an early hour, started for Merrygold Mansion. He had not journeyed far ere his heart began to beat with unusual violence, and he was compelled to adopt, by turns, all the ordinary antidotes of vulgar alarm, till the fund was entirely exhausted. Now he fervently declaimed against unmanliness and cowardice to dismal old oaks whose rustling leaves imparted a strange sort of quivering to his limbs which people are apt to mistake for manifestations of fear, then whistled and sung,—and sung and whistled again. It is true that there were a good many trills and quavers about his tones, but that might be owing to his ardent admiration of the Italian *recitativo*. At length, he arrived within sight of the dreadful spot. There it stood— the dismal black vault, here and there streaked by the shattered moonbeams with their pallid and trembling lines. Around it the pigmy copse wildly nodded its thin protruding branches to each whispering wind, whose continuous current broke the death-like stillness of the scene; while, at gloomy intervals, the long fern and mossy furze that fringed the dilapidated walls, waved, with drowsy motion, up and down, like evil spirits of the night. The schoolmaster hurried his step, bent upon contemplating as briefly as possible a spectacle which it was impracticable to avoid. With writhing contortions of frame he desperately advanced, imagining the most hideous shapes and figures in his path. Another instant would have placed him at a comfortable distance beyond the ruins, when a sharp whistle, whose shrill notes, painfully multiplied and prolonged, roused the deepest echoes of the wood into repetition, instantaneously surrounded him with, what appeared to his distempered fancy, innumerable spirits clad in robes of appalling whiteness. Rendered speechless from terror, our hero stood chained to the ground, while his red-plumed beaver displaced by the stiffened hair underneath whirled off his head, and speedily deposited itself in the mud.

With the first glimmer of returning consciousness Mr. Twiddle fell upon his knees, and devoutly supplicated the goblins to grant him his life.

"Oh! mighty spirits of the departed dead," he pompously commenced, "pity the humble being that kneels at your august feet."

"Presumptuous mortal!" gravely answered Hasleton; "what possessed thee to assume the seeming of a noble brother? Sisters, proceed on your holy task."

"O—h! oh!" growled Timothy in agony.

Armed with a pliant branchlet the first witch approached him, and thus commenced the weird chant:

> "Ye sisters big, and sisters small,
> Prepare to list unto our call,
> And switch this mortal one and all."

Thus singing she applied her lash to the schoolmaster, who bellowed like an ox at every fresh infliction, and was followed by the mystic sisterhood, repeating, as they imitated her example, the significant words,

> "Switch! Switch! Switch!
> Twitch! Twitch! Twitch!"

The first voice resumed :—

> " Now let him have it on the hip;
> Now make him dance—now make him skip—
> Quick bring the jack-knife that we rip ——"

" Jack-knife! you're going to rip me ?" shrieked the victim, in consternation and horror at the thought, applying his hands to that precious part of his body on which he conjectured the operation would be performed.   The instrument called for was soon produced by one of the subordinate sisters, and on its being placed in the first one's hand, she proceeded to cut off one of the skirts of his coat, which she adroitly attached to the end of her staff or wand, as a sort of trophy, singing the while,—

> " Pale sisters of the midnight moon
> That eat your meals with bloody spoon ——"

" The d—l you do," horridly grinned Timothy.

> " Advance ye now in charmed rows,
> And pluck this patriot by the nose."

" Pluck !" echoed the second sister, tugging at the victim's proboscis.

" Pluck ! pluck ! pluck !" severally repeated the others, imitating her example, unmoved by his piteous yells and screams.

When this part of the ceremony was concluded, she, who seemed the leader of the wizard band, approached him and spoke.

" Mortal," she solemnly said, " who have thus intruded into our sacred walks, and dared to disturb our nocturnal orgies, listen while I unfold thy irrevocable doom."

" Doom !" chattered the schoolmaster, despairingly; " they'll eat me—I know they will, the cannibals !"

" It is decreed that thou shalt dance a minuet," continued the speaker.

" Dance !" he ejaculated, " Oh, mighty spirit! I never danced in my life ——"

" Then, prepare," resumed the apparation, " prepare to ——"

" I'll dance !" shrieked out Timothy, fearful of the penalty his disobedience might incur.

At a given sign from the queen spirit, a lively air sounded from the bush.

" Begin !" cried a strange voice from the same quarter.

Trembling with agitation and fear, the schoolmaster commenced upon his new vocation. Faster and faster moved the playful measure—faster and faster shuffled the dancer's feet, executing a variety of steps equally remarkable for their ungracefulness and originality.   It was truly a novel and amusing spectacle to see a man impressed with the idea that the continuance of his life depended upon the agility of his feet.   But in Timothy's case this humourous suggestion was enhanced to inexpressible mirth by his ludicrous manifestations of alarm.   With one skirt of his disfigured coat floundering about at every eccentric motion of his crooked little body, his legs encumbered by jack boots of unusual dimensions, and his short, slender arms outstretched or contracted, turned in or turned out, just as increasing excitement prompted, he presented the happiest parody imaginable on the voluptuous graces of Terpsichore.   Indeed, so intent was he on doing justice to the character that circumstances had compelled him to assume, that when the hidden minstrel brought his dizzy measure to a close, his legs, arms, and feet, still continued their undefinable evolutions, as if the mere tendency of inertia effectually resisted every fresh volition.

" Man of earth," said the queen spirit, when he had finally succeeded in composing his refractory limbs, "we have watched the graceful movements of thy body"—here the spirit paused—it is conjectured to laugh. "Pleased with thy prompt obedience," she resumed, "we were, a moment past, resolved in the plenitude of our graciousness and clemency, upon according thee thy life and freedom; but reports have reached our ears that thou hast often scandalised our holy sisterhood by such foul names as Night Witches, Scare-crows, and Hags. We would confront thee with thy accuser—let him appear."

This part having been allotted in the general distribution of characters to the convivial student, he tottered forth, notwithstanding he had forgotten every word of it, from his tree, where his time had been beguiled and his spirits exhilarated by frequent appeals to the contents of a small flask which he carried in his pocket.

"Proceed," said the spirit.

"Pro-ro-ro-ceed! ha! ha! he! he! you do-do-don't say—I ain't a witch. I'm a Indian—Yahou! hou! hou! Yahou! Lo-o-o-o-k here, boys, let's duck this fellow in the pond."

"Agreed," answered the others, who were growing tired of the farce.

"Oh! most potent spirits!—oh! most etherial fairies!" screamed Mr. Twiddle, as they rushed upon him *en masse*, and lifted him up by the shoulders and feet, from the ground.

Thus supported, they hurried him, without farther ceremony, to the pond, where, after swinging him up and down with shouts of boisterous hilarity, he was pitched, headforemost, into the water, while the mischievous elves hastily retreated.

Leaving the hapless wight to extricate himself as best he may from his unfortunate dilemma, we return to Edward St. Julian and his singular guide. After following for a long time in her stately but rapid footsteps through the mazy windings of the forest, a bright illumination at last glimmered through intervening tree and foliage upon his sight. Judging from the different paths he had taken, and the appearance of the spot over which he was now conducted by his guide, the young man concluded that it shone from Merry-gold Mansion; a suspicion which was not a little strengthened by the sounds of revelry that occasionally met his ears, and which was ultimately confirmed by their approach within sight of a familiar garden that surrounded the dwelling. The strange figure entered it by a little wicket, whose broken latch scarcely offered any resistance, and directing her steps to one of the nearest arbours which had been erected for the joyful occasion, paused suddenly at the entrance, and beckoned him in. The gesture was no sooner made than complied with, when the young man discovered to his infinite surprise that a third party already occupied the bower. This was a domino, whose loose garb betrayed the soft outline of a female form, and who sat in an attitude of pensive dejection and grief. She cast a hasty glance upon the new comers as they entered, but did not speak.

"I go no farther—what means all this?" inquired Edward, turning abruptly upon the singular being who had him led to this spot.

The domino started with apparent astonishment from her seat at the sound of his voice; but the motion was too sudden and transient either to attract observation or awaken curiosity.

"I mean," answered the guide, lifting her hand with an air of authority, "that at this point, with a few words, we must part. The person you behold is the being I have described."

Edward St. Julian scrutinised, for the first time, his co-inmate of the harbour, and, with the searching penetration of love, at once recognised in the stranger's fragile pro

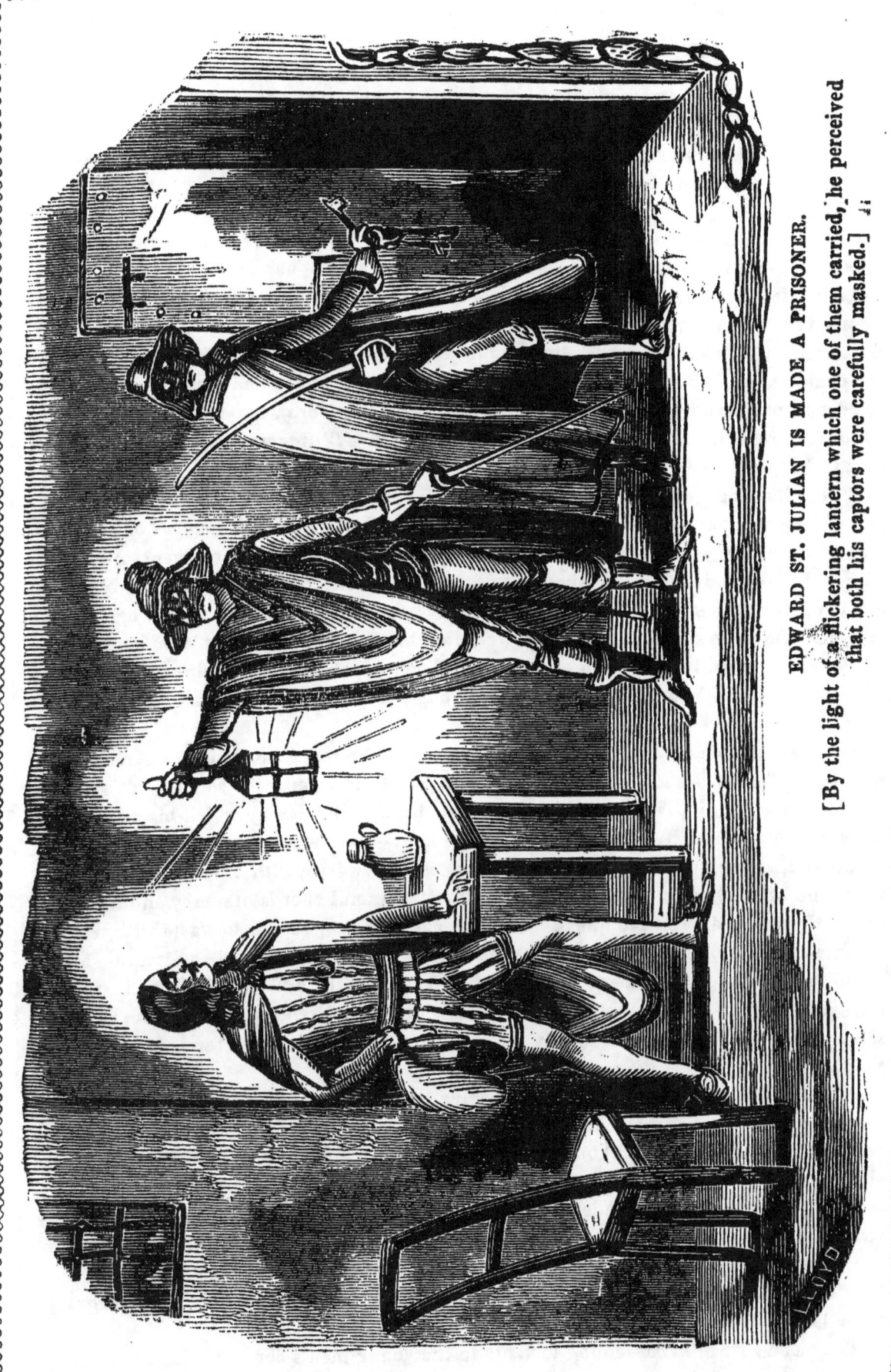

EDWARD ST. JULIAN IS MADE A PRISONER.

[By the light of a flickering lantern which one of them carried, he perceived that both his captors were carefully masked.]

portions, and a hand, which was half revealed by the heavy folds of her sable robe, Rosalind's beautiful daughter.

"It is she!" he mentally ejaculated—"*it is she!*"

"Lady," said the speaker, in low but distinct tones, "it is not for me to speak of your affection for this youth ——"

"Hold!" proudly exclaimed Blanche (for it was she), half rising from her mossy seat.

"Nay, interrupt me not," continued the other, imperiously; "I have that to speak on which your life, and, what is much dearer than life, your happiness, depends. You have been basely bartered, and, with to-morrow's sun, will be sacrificed to an outlaw and a villain. Avoid the man you call your father. Remember—beware!"

Filled with indignation at what she mistakenly deemed a vile subterfuge to mislead her from duty, and to prevent the accomplishment of the promise she had given her father, she immediately rose to her feet, bent upon exposing the shameless falsehood; but, ere she could collect her senses sufficiently for the effort, the figure had disappeared, and she stood up, musing on its beckoning hand and vanishing form, like one lost in a dream; while the prophetic admonition, "*Remember me—beware!*" lingered with painful distinctness in her ears.

While thus engaged, the wrapper, or gown, she wore, was partly thrown open, and her graceful form, arrayed in more comely habits, was thus displayed to the eyes of her lover, who had scarcely yet recovered from the emotions of mingled amazement and terror with which she had heard the apparition's warning. All the fervour of his quiescent passion returned, as he dwelt upon the lovely maiden. Her arm rested against the foliaged frame-work of the artificial bower, and her fair neck and shoulders, exposed by her fallen hood, which had been accidentally displaced, shone like sculptured marble in a bright stream of moonlight that escaped through the rustling leaves and branches overhead.

There are moments in life when the allurements of temptation cannot be resisted or repelled. This was such an one to Edward St. Julian; and he sought, in vain, to repress the kindling desires which awoke in his breast, and before which his past resolutions melted, as frost in the sunshine. It was she!—she, whom he had meanly deserted to satisfy the cravings of that sordid passion which sweeps with iron finger the holiest affections of the heart; which snaps asunder its tuneful chords of mercy and love, and leaves the deluded wretch to quake with the pangs of remorse, or to waste with tears of repentance;—she, the loved, the lost one, whom he had fascinated to discard—bewildered to betray. His father's wrongs—his fearful oath, and the fatal obligations it imposed—all—all were forgotten in that short but signal triumph of the lover over the son; and, throwing himself wildly at her feet, he passionately and fervently exclaimed:—

"Blanche, dearest Blanche, can you forgive me?"

"Rise, sir," firmly answered the girl, who regarded what had transpired as a snare to entrap and deceive her, and thought she beheld its wily author in the supplicant—"rise, sir; you have sunk low enough, and need not abase yourself the more."

"No, Blanche,—no!" he despairingly cried, clasping her hand, which she violently struggled to disengage, closer and closer within his own; "you will not despise and spurn one who entreats for pity and pardon."

"The former, sir, you have," she replied, freeing herself with an effort from his grasp; "the last you may never obtain."

The blood rushed in consuming torrents to the young man's cheeks, as he bounded up, trembling in every fibre with that indomitable pride which had set its fatal seal of identity upon his fathers.

"If to have sunk so low, Miss Rosalind," he answered, "merits only your compassion, I must blush for my temporary abasement, while I sincerely grieve, for your sake, that one so young and artless should so soon have learnt to violate in practice the divine precepts which she professes to respect in principle."

"Would that were all you might justly blush for," said the maiden, tremulously, stealing a glance at his noble form, and proudly curling lip, rendered more bitter by the uncertain light in which it was viewed, and stamping him a descendant of the haughty race to which he was allied by parity of nature and of name. "Was it generous, sir," continued Blanche, "to resort to so base an artifice in order to deceive an unwary female, and counteract her dutiful inclinations?"

"Artifice! I do not apprehend you, miss," said the astonished youth.

"It is in vain, Edward St. Julian, that you affect to misconceive my meaning. Artifice was the word, and what means this empty parade of opposition and warning, if it be not to alarm and subdue an unsuspecting heart? Oh! Edward, Edward—that I should live to despise you."

"By all that is sacred, you wrong me," said the young man, eagerly. "Heaven knows ——"

"Stop, sir!" she exclaimed, in a tone of authority, "Heaven will not bear false witness. You knew, sir, that my troth was plighted to another."

"Plighted to another!" he echoed, wildly, starting forward and grasping her hand firmly. "Speak, Blanche Rosalind," he added, with chilling composure, "do you say the truth?"

"You know it," she calmly replied. "What means this?"

"Come, now," he said, laughing with the morbid incredulity of madness, "this is a bitter joke—you do not mean it, say so."

"Release me, sir."

"Speak!—speak!" was whispered in a choking voice.

"Nay—unhand me," answered the maiden, seeking to extricate herself; "it is sinful. You know that to-morrow will see me the sworn bride of another—I beseech you—in the name of manhood—my last request—cruel—cruel—*I command you, sir, to release my hand!*"

It was instantaneously dropped.

"The man that weds you, Blanche Rosalind," vehemently exclaimed the youth, "shall first set a victor's heel upon my fallen crest; I swear it! as I hope for mercy here, and salvation hereafter."

Heedless of the maiden's condition, who had fallen back upon her seat, the speaker darted forth from the bower, and took a path leading to the main road.

He had advanced but a short distance when two men started up, suddenly, from opposite sides of the path, seized upon him, from behind, and blindfolded his eyes.

"Cowards!" he screamed out, struggling desperately with the ruffians. "You will pay for this anon."

No reply was made to his loud threats and imprecations, and he was conducted in silence by a circuitous route which caution, doubtless, suggested to his escort, to prevent any difficulties which might arise from a subsequent recognition of the way by their prisoner. Arrived at the point of destination, the fillet, or band, was removed from his face, and he was ushered into a gloomy suite of apartments in some unknown building, whose grated windows and dusky furniture presented a most forlorn and cheerless aspect.

He had only time to remark, by the light of a flickering lantern which one of them carried, that his captors were carefully masked, when the heavy door was abruptly closed upon him, and the loud turns of its ponderous locks, accompanied by a noise of bolts and bars, announced that he was a captive, without furnishing any clue to the probable cause of his captivity.

CHAPTER XI.

Wilt thou reach stars, because they shine on thee?
Go, base intruder! overweening slave!
*   *   *   *   *   *
And think, my patience, more than thy desert,
Is privileged for thy departure hence.
Thank me for this, more than for all the favours
Which, all too much, I have bestowed on thee.
Two Gentlemen of Verona.

ON the next morning, Rosalind and his Italian guest were seated together in the former's private apartment. The reader is aware that this inauspicious day was fixed upon to consummate the daughter's heroic sacrifice of her hand and heart to her crafty parent's security, a circumstance which will render us more intelligible when we go on to state that Marcello's looks, unlike those of his moody companion, were unusually cheerful and gay. His dress, too, though a morning habit or dishabille only, was arranged with the most scrupulous neatness, and showed that, albeit his morals had degenerated in a bad school, his taste, at least, had entirely escaped its contagious influence.

"Think you it was she?" inquired Rosalind, by way of reviving the conversation, which was at this time labouring under the effects of a dull pause.

"I think, signor, but am not certain; there is precious little charity in this world. Our eyes as well as our ears may be deceived. For my part, I wouldn't assume to be certain of anything if I were the representative of St. Peter on earth, and had red-nosed bishops to hold up my train, and plump-looking cardinals to take care of my hat."

"You treat this matter with unbecoming lightness, perhaps," seriously remarked Rosalind, chafing his brow thoughtfully; then, assuming a disinterested and friendly air, he added, "pray, relate all the incidents—the suspicion may be true, after all; my mind, being freer than yours at this moment, I will be better able to hear them, and, if expedient, make preparations for any danger that may be reasonably apprehended."

"Danger! Santa Maria! Signor Rosalind, you are particular as an old crow with her poultry. However, if you will hear it, thus it is:—Ere we met the figure a second time, and locked up that spirited youth underneath, who was bent upon sending me to my brother saints before my time, I observed it in the ball-room. As the strange thing glided past, methought I saw through the tresses of its long black hair a chain very much resembling that of my damsel aboard the brigantine: so I followed it, in hopes of discovering Lauretta in the masquerading mummer. But, St. Francis witness my word, she was too shrewd for me, and fixed her veil so that my head was left as wise as my feet. I now lost sight of her for awhile, and again discerned her beckoning the fair mistress of my heart to the place in which we afterwards found the last in conversation with that young cur. This I deemed a mere trick of character, and, therefore, troubled myself not a whit more about it until I met you, and we proceeded to seek her out. She's a witch, signor, or we would have been more successful, after all our trouble and fatigue, than to arrive, as we did, just in time to see her disappear. This is all—Heaven and you see the danger, for I do not."

" Yet I am still disposed to think more gravely of the matter than you," remarked Rosalind. " It may be Lauretta, and if so ———"

" What then ?" interrupted the smuggler ; "what then, signor? I care not—for the wretch knows me, and my temper, too, I trow. Rob! signor—to play a bold game requires a bold hand. You are too scary. Let the clowns be nice who dance at fandangos—I'm not of the craft."

Here a domestic announced that the morning meal was served up. Marcello carefully rose, and followed him, humming as he went an old ballad of his native land. Rosalind was on the point of imitating his good example when Lucy the housekeeper entered.

" A word, if you have time," she briefly said to her master.

" Certainly, Lucy, certainly," he answered, in the bland and honeyed tones of voice which he sometimes assumed.

" Old subject," continued the Jezabel, drily; " my reward. I have waited a year—two years—three years—you can count. It is time ; marriage! money! you know the promise."

" My dear Lucy, all will come in due time," resumed Rosalind. " It is true, I promised to marry you, and likewise to give the sum required for your relatives ; but at present my affairs are in so very embarrassed a state that—that—in fine, I only regret that I am inevitably compelled to delay an event which would confer as much happiness upon myself as it would, doubtless, yield satisfaction to you."

" Eh!" screeched the housekeeper with an incredulous look. " Flattery—I know all —Marcello—Blanche. It must be done to-day. Patience—ha! ha! worn out."

" I can only repeat," said her master, somewhat provoked at her obstinacy, which, however, he yet expected to overcome, as usual, by fair speeches and additional promises—" I can only repeat what I have just spoken—with the best will in the world, my circumstances forbid it."

" Do they?" quietly answered the hag, grinning till her protruding teeth were painfully visible ; " you know the penalty."

" You do not mean that, surely ?" inquired Rosalind, with the humility of a supplicant.

" I do," was the emphatic reply.

He paced the floor moodily, turning now and then to the aged crone to notice whether her wrinkled visage betrayed the slightest hope of compromise or conciliation ; but it still remained stern and inflexible as that of the rigid boatman of Styx, of which, indeed, it was, otherwise, no indifferent a similitude.

" Are you fully resolved upon this course ?" he at length demanded, pausing and knitting his brows together darkly, as if some dreadful purpose laboured in his mind.

" Ay."

" See you play the game skillfully, then," he fiercely retorted. " Mark me, my honesty alone makes the fulfilment of this promise obligatory upon me. I never did—I do not fear you, now. The story," he continued, glancing at her keenly, as if he intended the expression of his features to be a commentary upon his language—" the story of itself would send you to the madhouse."

" You say so; ay! understand you." Her gray eyes sparkled with a glance of tenfold defiance.

"Well!" he eagerly added, astonished at her unyielding stubbornness.

"My brother lives. Ha! ha! Your memory does not always serve you," cried the beldame, wildly. This was the longest sentence he had ever heard from her lips.

For awhile Rosalind seemed chained to the ground; but as the tiger goaded to his lair turns with renewed vigour and ferocity upon his foe, the clouds gathered darker and darker upon his brow, and his fingers, by degrees, were spasmodically closed, as he hastily strode forward, and exclaimed, in a burst of ungovernable wrath, "Vile wretch! I despise thy arts and thee!"

"Do it, *now?*" asked Lucy, tauntingly.

"No!" he shouted in reply. "Miserable hag! thy schemes are not so sure but they may be foiled! Look to it."

"This evening, then—for my brothers," screamed the housekeeper, threateningly.

"Speak it louder still," answered Rosalind—"that the walls may mock thy dismal croaking, as my power shall crush thy grasping impotence. Go!—seek thy minion—drivelling dotard, begone!"

His finger pointed to the door as he spoke these words, and his firm-set teeth and flashing eyeballs plainly indicated the violent passions that were struggling in his bosom.

For the first time the shrivelled old crone shrunk from his terrible glance.

The injunction was not repeated; but a startling sound, produced by his heavy boot, which was impatiently brought to the floor, sufficed to dismiss the treacherous accomplice from his presence.

CHAPTER XII.

—— While the wings of Fancy still are free,
And I can view this mimic show of thee,
Time has but half succeeded in his theft ——
Thyself removed, thy power to soothe me left.—COWPER.

THE day after his entertainment, Mr. Merrygold, assisted by little Nora, busied himself in arranging the furniture of his dwelling, which had been thrown into a state of sad disorder and confusion by his masquerading guests. After setting to right the commodious moveables, which, besides fulfilling their immediate purposes of convenience and comfort, served to embellish the spacious apartments that they occupied, he directed his labours to the destruction of numerous artificial beauties with which his garden and lawn had been disfigured for the occasion, and, finally, marched in triumph, at the dinner bell's joyful summons, over the mutilated fragments of dismantled arches and desolated groves. Arrived at the house, he sat down with his youthful companion, to partake of the frugal refection that awaited them; an operation which he performed without those occasional anecdotes and sallies of wit, with which he was wont to enliven the maiden at such times. It is scarcely necessary to observe, that this unusual taciturnity was produced by the fatigues of the morning, which had contributed in no small degree to sharpen an appetite that his healthy constitution and temperate habits rendered naturally quite keen enough to dispense with all extrinsic stimulants.

"Ah! that's comfortable," he said, in his usual abrupt but good-natured voice, rising from the table and clearing his throat—"What do you say to it, my child, eh? Why, you have eat nothing, Nora. It won't do, child—there—there, now—no, it won't! You must eat, my little ferret—eating is necessary to life—you ought to have heard Jenkins on that subject—a great political economist that! Eating, he said one day to

Lady Tinsel, eating, your ladyship, is necessary to labour, and labour is the great—there I am now,—talking to you about what you can't understand—just like an old fool—so I am—well—well !"

"Father," said Nora, " you promised to tell me about that handsome lady in the picture if I was a good little girl—haven't I been good ?"

"So you have, by Jove! who disputes it?" replied the old gentleman. "Odds bodkins !—I'll do it—so I will."

He approached the door of the cabinet, and thrusting his hand into his pocket, drew out a diminutive key of curious make and construction. This he was preparing to apply, when the door, which he had forgotten to secure the day before, was suddenly opened by the weight of little Nora's body, who, missing her foothold, leaned against it for support in the emergency.

"There child, you've hurt yourself, I know it," exclaimed the naturalist, who felt for her all the scrupulous solicitude of parental love, extending his arms towards the girl, and assisting to obstruct her fall.

"No, sir, I'm not hurt. Oh! look at the door, it's open," she anxiously exclaimed, pointing to the door.

"So it is," he answered, observing it now for the first time, and gaping with astonishment at the unaccountable phenomenon.

" The people last night, perhaps," suggested Nora, by way of affording a solution to the mystery.

"The people !" echoed the naturalist, slightly irritated, entering into the cabinet, and looking round eagerly to see whether any object had been displaced or injured. " Yes—no !" he added, doubtfully ; " they wouldn't do it—odds fish ! they wouldn't be so mean. Come into my cabinet. If I were to catch any man spoiling my collection, I'd kill—no, I wouldn't kill, but I'd beat—shaw, I'm a jack, I wouldn't beat either, for it might be accident—but—I'd cry, child—yes, I'd cry for the poor dumb things. I love them, you see, very much ; so I do."

The old man's voice slightly trembled as he spoke these words, and he almost wept with joy to observe, after a minute survey of his curiosity shop, that it had suffered no disparagement whatever from the accident.

" You'll never love me like you love them," said Nora, turning her dark and expressive orbs upon him with a sad but affectionate look. " They say mothers love their little girls so much," she added ; " oh ! how I wish I had a mother."

" There, child, that's the third time you've said that. I don't like it ; no, I don't. You know I prize you more than these foolish things, but then—they are old friends—old friends shouldn't be forgotten. And it wouldn't be strange if I were to lose them, either. There's Rose, though she didn't love me, but what's that to me—I loved her—well, she's dead. Then, there is my dog Jenkins ; I called him after Jenkins, poor fellow ! he cared for me too, for when he died, he called me to his death-bed, and taking me by the hand, he said, ' Merrygold, you've been my friend ; I'm going on my long journey, good bye.' They gave me the animal that very day. Well, he was always by me, like his namesake, never out of sight when I wanted comfort or consolation. You've seen his grave in the garden. I go there sometimes, and think on him. Poor creature, he used to jump about and caress me in the morning, and lick my hand and wag his tail—so he did. And when he died—just like his namesake, you see—he crawled up to me, for he was too weak to walk, and gave me his paw,—then—then he left his old master for ever. If there's a heaven, he's gone to it—I know it—I know it."

As these painful associations recurred to his mind in rapid and melancholy succession, the old man's sensibilities were deeply moved. His words grew almost inaudible as he incoherently concluded, and a shower of tears, which he vainly endeavoured to repress, burst spontaneously from his eyes. Little Nora sprang upon her chair which stood behind him, and with the eloquent instinct of her young but feeling heart, dwelt with the touching earnestness of childish sympathy upon his face. It is true, he did not speak, but his countenance was not averted as usual at such times from her glance, nor was any other sign of similar import made. Her endearing caress, however, did not pass without a grateful acknowledgment of the relief it afforded, and a transient pressure of her throbbing breast to his own, assured the orphan that it was not overlooked and would never be forgotten.

"Father," she said, wiping his cheeks with a handkerchief, which she drew with some exertion out of his great coat; "never mind about that story of the lady in the picture. I know it will make you feel bad, because sometimes, when you don't know I'm by, I see you looking at it for a long time, as if it made you think of things that make people cry."

"Pshaw, child! do you take me for an old woman?" answered Mr. Merrygold, striving to assume his ordinary cheerfulness, and shaking his powdered head significantly. "I'll tell you the whole story from beginning to end. Zounds! I don't weep once in an age. When I was grand secretary of the Royal Entomological and Zoological Society, I was thought a man of nerve—so I was. There—sit down, you little fairy—now—that's comfortable!"

He paused a few seconds as if to refresh his memory by reflection, and then proceeded, in his brief style, to narrate the history of his own life, in which that of the mysterious portrait was involved.

"I never knew my father—he was dead before I came into the world. I was an only child, and my mother's affection was great enough to ruin a thousand children. I went to college when I was sixteen, and fought a pitch battle with Greek and Latin for four years. Perhaps you don't know what I call Greek and Latin—how could you? Two kinds of gibberish those who talk don't understand, and those who understand can't talk—that's it; now you know as much of the matter as I do. My mother had a sister who married a man in humbler circumstances than my father. What was the consequence? I had an army of cousins—poor people always have plenty of children. Do you know what a cousin is, child? A cousin is a relation who only remembers the relationship when you can do him a favour. If he's rich—he'll see you in gown and slippers at breakfast or in his bed-room; if poor, he boards at your house, and is always prodigiously affectionate and hungry—that's a cousin. Zounds! it isn't a curiosity, or I'd have one in my collection. There are innumerable species embraced in the genus and—there now!—what an old fool I am—using scientific terms to a child—odds fish! just like me. All my cousins hated me because I went through college and had my name written in crooked letters on a kind of paper they call parchment, and signed by a crowd of old fellows who wore tremendous periwigs, and spoilt their handwritings to pass for great men. My cousins were all tradesmen and clerks. Child, I'm going to tell you something very serious—you mustn't speak it again;" at this stage of the narrative the speaker's countenance grew suddenly grave, and he seemed to hesitate if he should continue it or no. "The fact is—Zounds! I was a fool—I fell in love with one of my cousins—she was an angel! I said so—swore it on the family Bible—and her mother agreed with me perfectly—mothers always agree on that point. But somehow or

THE DARK DEED IN THE OLD SANCTUARY.

[She felt the grasp of an iron hand upon her, and a glittering object flitted across her vision.]

other she said—that is—I don't know that she thought so, either—but she said that my feelings were not reciprocated—yes! *not reciprocated* were the words—so they were. It was a hard blow, child, and I felt it—yet still I cheered up—odds fish! as I always do under misfortune—looking at the bright side of the picture—hoping for better things. Time, I said to myself—time will unite us—but alas! three weeks after my first proposal we were separated—for ever.—Wheugh! how my cheeks are perspiring." Here the speaker applied his handkerchief to his face with an equivocal sort of twitch that, together with his faltering voice, seemed to indicate a different cause for the movement. "Yes," he resumed in a firmer tone, "three weeks afterwards her father took it into his head to leave the mother country for a wilderness—and sailed for America. Of course she followed her parents. You're thinking now that I felt bad about it—so I did. But I was a philosopher—impenetrable as adamant, as poor Jenkins once said in his great speech at the club. A few years after I was elected grand secretary of our Association. Egad! I was proud of the distinction—who wouldn't have been? The whole family were proud of it. Lady Tinsel shook her fan at me knowingly—and smiled so beautifully that all her small white teeth were made visible (she never did so except on extraordinary occasions); and even aunt Primrose—prim and precious as she was, the old dear thing—winked at me—ha!—ha!—odds fish! it was so, winked at the grand secretary of the Royal Entomological and Zoological Society! Who knows but Rose would have—there I am talking of her again! What's she to me? Nothing—nothing, only I've got her picture, that's all—you see, that's all. You asked me how I obtained it—there, child, I see it in your face; well, that's what I have been coming at all this while. My aunt left her miniature with my mother, and Jenkins copied it on canvass. Not at my solicitation though—what would I want with a woman's likeness? pshaw! It was a beautiful head piece and so he fancied it. I kept it in remembrance of the artist. As for the original I never think of—yes, child, don't believe me, I am an old liar—there now, don't talk about it! Zounds! I'm travelling out of my story. Some years after they had left the mother country, I determined to follow their example. They had settled in South Carolina, and hither I came. I had some strong notions of meeting *her* again, foolish thought!—the family were scattered about Heaven knows where when I arrived, and she ——"

"Was dead!" eagerly interrupted Nora, observing the shade which suddenly stole over his placid brow at this moment.

"Dead!—yes, child, she was—there!—I'm lying again, she was not dead, but *lost!* lost to honour and to me; she was disgraced. You don't understand me and I can't explain, but so it was.—Zounds! I'm getting excited for nothing—just like me!"

Observing that the maiden appeared doubtful as to the import of the last few words, Mr. Merrygold terminated his story by an expressive though brief commentary upon their meaning, which he did not fail to accompany with several sagacious reflections on the moral tendency of his cousin's failing, in order that she might, in future, profit by the melancholy example thus impressed upon her mind.

"Here," he said, in conclusion, alluding to the spot on which he resided, "here I have remained ever since. All alone, without anything to care for, just like a stuffed bird or dried reptile. And that dark man Rosalind right under my nose too—they say he *did it*—but that may be a tale, so it may; still I hate to be his neighbour. Well, well, my little girl, I won't complain either. This world is a world of thorns and briers, and we must expect to be scratched and bruised in getting through it. Heaven has blest me at last—so it has, with a daughter, a likely daughter. Egad! I'm beginning to be as proud as when Jenkins first slapped me on the shoulder, and said, 'Merrygold, I congratulate you, you dog—grand secretary of the Royal Entomological and Zoological Society.' Ha! ha! I had my spirits then—poor fellow! he's dead now, and the dog too—pshaw! you see, child, I am an old fool, everything is for the better, so it is."

"Oh! father!" cried Nora, glancing towards the window; "you see Mr. St. Julian's man running across the lawn? I'll go and ask what he wants."

"Yes, my child, go; and if he won't come in, the rascal, don't forget to ask about Ned. Odds bodkins!" he added, to himself, as the little Nora started upon her errand, "he's a fine fellow, that—so he is! Who would have thought he knew more about butterflies than I? I'll bequeath him my collection and my manuscript of observations; I know he'll prize the one and publish the other—so he will, he's a man of taste."

The young girl returned shortly after, but with a countenance that betokened feelings far different from those with which she had left the apartment.

"Father—father," she exclaimed at her entrance—"Edward St. Julian is lost!"

"Lost!" echoed the old gentleman, starting up with amazement from his chair; "Ned lost? how? It's a trick, you little fairy—I see it!—no, no, you're serious. Ned St. Julian lost! Give me my hat and cane! It can't be lost—lost—odds fish! I'll ransack the country, so I will. Ned—lost—pshaw! I don't believe it—not a word of it—quick, child!"

Hastily seizing upon the objects called for, with which he was speedily furnished by little Nora, he hurried out of his house, and directed his steps towards the evil messenger, who, with the characteristic stoicism and unconcern of his menial tribe, stood conversing with one of his brother servants in front of the kitchen door.

CHAPTER XIII.

Duke. Woman, stand forth;
Nay, cast away thy veil—look on her, Fazio.
Faz. Bianca!—No, it is a horrid vision;
And, if I struggle, I shall wake and find it
A miscreated mockery of the brain.

* * * * *

It was not well, Bianca, in my guilt,
To cut me off—thus early—thus unripe. *Fazio—a Tragedy.*

WHEN the hapless hour at length arrived in which Blanche Rosalind was to unite her earthly destinies to those of the sordid wretch, whom a parent's safety had alone commended to her magnanimous choice, she was seated at her casement absorbed in a fit of profound but subdued meditation. A heavenly radiance shone from her mild blue eyes, which alternately glanced, with the sudden movement of intense thought, from the landscape to the sky, or seemed to watch, through a natural break in the intervening oaks and pines, the spray-crested billows that rolled beyond. It may be that her hands, which rested carelessly upon her lap, and the backward inclination of her person, might betoken the sullen despondency of grief, but no shadows dimmed her delicate brow, which rather indicated the placid composure of devotion, than the brooding apathy of despair. Yet was there a struggle in that fair one's heart which all the energy of filial veneration could not entirely suppress; a struggle that originated in a rash resolve to crush even the recollection of what had once animated her life, and to merge the sad twilight of a hopeless love in the more dismal prospect of an inflexible duty. Nor was this the effect of a bigoted enthusiasm, or an overstrained perception of right, but the suggestion of principles which, though rigid to a fault, were proportionately liberal and enlightened. Alas! she had not yet fully estimated the magnitude of the task she had undertaken to perform. They know little of the human heart who imagine that the chain of its early affections may be rudely sundered or readily unwound. It is a despotism whose sway is deeply rooted in the fondest associations of the past; and though resembling, indeed, the frail floweret of spring—that a passing breath may shatter, or a dew-drop overweigh—in the prismatic brilliancy of its hues, yet withstands the cares and viscissitudes of life, and is imperishable as the earth itself, from which the floweret shoots. It is with us from the beginning, and endures with us to the end. Canopied in these dreamy remembrances of departed bliss, that soothe in disease and console in sorrow, its flow is perpetual; and when the morning of a higher existence sheds its opening light on the benighted pilgrim of this, the last star that lingers over Memory's waste, is the first-born of fancy—the fresh Love of youth! It was this passion that the maiden had promised to conquer, and which now obstinately resisted her most determined efforts. She had succeeded, indeed, in the task of self-denial, which duty demanded at her hands; but she could not summon the sacrilegious fortitude to crush the faded blossoms she had already consigned to its bier. Thoughts of her Edward — so worshipped in the wild idolatry of a virgin heart—momentarily flashed across her vision, as if to make ruin more appalling; and though her lips moved not, and her fore-head semed undisturbed and calm, there was a shock of the elements within more dreadful for being still, speechless, and concentrated. Why were the rich trappings that adorned her person? For what end was the garland of pure white flowers so carefully enwreathed, that lay beside her? Flowers for the bride—flowers for the bridal! Ay—she shuddered as she thought—there are flowers for the dead.

She had continued in this morbid frame of mind for a few brief instants when a clock in the corner struck six, and a servant almost immediately entered the apartment. It was her chamber-maid, or *femme d'atours*, bearing a lamp in her hand. The shadows of evening were gathering fast, and the spot occupied by the maiden now afforded a view of the sun, which, like a magnificent fire-ball, was rapidly sinking amid his peaks and cliffs of variable azure, fringed with crimson and pearl, into his woodland canopy.

"All is ready; they only wait upon you, madam," said the domestic.

She rose from her seat, and approached the toilet-table, that her maid might more conveniently adjust the bridal chaplet to its destined place. Not a word fell from her lips—not a tear was in her eye—and her features, with the composure, had all the stiffness of marble. This done, the servant led the way, and she followed in her quick footsteps with the unfaltering firmness of a martyr. Such is the strength of the female heart, when its latent energies are stimulated to activity by the kindred calls of duty and honour.

After traversing several of the spacious apartments in which Rosalind mansion abounded, they finally reached the great hall, in which it was settled that the marriage rites should be performed. It was magnificently decorated with festoons of artificial greenery, gracefully suspended from column to column, and illuminated by candelabras of dazzling lusture and various dye. At one extremity of the hall were placed two velvet cushions, side by side, which were ornamented with golden fringe and thick embroidery. Fronting these was a curiously-worked table, supporting a massive astral lamp, at which were seated two middle-aged men, whose characteristic habits intimated that they were the lawyer and priest. The bridegroom stood within a few paces of the table, and was arrayed in a suit whose elegance became the occasion and the objects around. He stepped forward as Blanche approached, and extended his hand, which she accepted with all desirable readiness.

"If the parties are ready," said the notary, rising from his seat, and inclining his head respectfully—movements which his companion did not fail to imitate—"we will proceed to sign the contract. Your father, miss," he added, addressing himself to the bride, whose looks plainly denoted her surprise at his absence; "your father has desired me to say that he is too indisposed to leave his chamber, which he is compelled to keep by sudden weakness and debility of body. Will it please you now to proceed?" She nodded an assent, and in proper time appended her signature to the parchment with a degree of decision and firmness, which, inasmuch as it appeared bold for the delicacy of her position, was, on that account, ill-calculated to excite any suspicion of the secret anguish she experienced.

This being the signal for commencing the imposing ceremony which it was the minister's duty to perform, he accordingly rose from his seat, and directing the bride and bridegroom to kneel, began the customary exhortations with much solemnity of manner. As he concluded this part of the ceremonial, and proceeded to propose those vital interrogatories which in all happy connexions have been anticipated by the ardour of reciprocal affection, the few persons who were present, being the servants of the mansion and some of their relatives, drew closer and closer to each other, and whispers of "How pale she is! Heavens, she will faint!" were almost distinctly audible, as they rapidly passed from mouth to mouth. The holy man had now reached the last stage. Like the spectators, his interest in the ceremony seemed to increase with its proximity to the end, and his voice, therefore, grew deeper and deeper in his progress. At length came the breathless close: "If any man can show just cause why they may not lawfully be joined together,"—here a confused hum of voices at the hall door was heard. The speaker paused, but reassuring himself with a glance, resumed—"let him now speak, or hereafter for ever hold his peace."

These words were no sooner pronounced than the door of the great hall was suddenly thrown open, and the tumult discovered to proceed from the mansion servants, who were vainly exerting themselves to obstruct the entrance of a little man in black, who had all the external insignificance of a subordinate functionary of the law, and several of his surly deputies following close at his heels.

The menials now prudently gave way, and the new comers marched up the hall towards the matrimonial party, while all stood waiting, in mute and breathless astonishment, the issue of this unexpected interruption.

"I arrest you in the name of the state," said the little man in black, drawing himself up to his utmost height, and assuming all the dignity of his office at once. "You are the captain of the brigantine." This was accompanied with an emphatic stroke of his hand upon the bridegroom's shoulder, which had the double effect of fulfilling a customary form and of awakening the latter from a state of half-stupor into which his amazement had thrown him.

"Par la Madona! thou shalt fight for it!" he cried out, starting to his feet, and waving a bright stiletto which he drew from his bosom with the celerity of light.

"Officers, do your duty!" said the magistrate, in no wise dissuaded from his purpose by this show of resistance, and stepping aside to give them place.

The Italian struggled manfully for a few seconds, but overcome by the superiority of numbers, he finally surrendered and was immediately pinioned and otherwise secured by the officers.

"Minions!" he exclaimed, as he underwent this disgraceful process; "it is a lie! By all the infernal spirits, ye and your papers lie! Who is my accuser?"

"I," answered a strange voice to the question. Every eye was at once turned upon the speaker, a female habited in robes of white, whose face was denied to the view by a thick black veil, and who stood forth from the crowd as if she had suddenly dropped from the clouds.

"Who are you?" vociferated the ruffian.

She made no reply, but hastily removed the veil from her countenance.

"Lauretta! You could have done this?" cried the prisoner, starting back aghast, a if he gazed on an unearthly apparition.

"Ay!" answered his treacherous mistress—for it was she—darting upon him a look of defiance and triumph that seemed to penetrate his very soul; " look you, proud bandit of the seas—our bond is cancelled—the betrayed is the betrayer now!"

A graceful motion of her hand, and the public functionary marshalled the prisoner and his escort to a spot adjoining the door. The stranger woman paused and whispered in Blanche's ears, "I told you to beware!" then moved towards the party of which she appeared to be the leader, who filed out of the arched portal as soon as she had reached them.

All had now recovered from the shock, except the intended bride. Her hands were still united together as if the marriage ceremony had not been broken off; her lips were hermetically sealed, and the expression of her eyes was unsettled and wild. She seemed to have lost the faculty of speech, and resembled, in her motionless beauty, the spirit of an eastern dream.

But this could not endure long; and tears at length flooded her pale cheeks, as she hysterically muttered a few inaudible words, and fell back senseless on the embroidered cushion, where recently knelt the tyrant from whose power she felt herself released for ever by the timely interposition of Heaven.

CHAPTER XVI.

> What woman is she,
> So wrinkled and old?
>
> *Thalaba, the Destroyer, by* SOUTHEY.

> If it were done, when 'tis done, 'twere well
> It were done quickly. *Macbeth.*

LUCY had scarce retired from the apartment, when Rosalind's features were distorted into one of those unnatural smiles which only visited his countenance when some hideous purpose was labouring in his mind. For a while he paced the chamber up and down with impatient and disordered steps, then abruptly pausing and folding his arms, muttered something between his teeth, in which the housekeeper's name was emphatically mingled. It is evident that this woman, like the rapacious foreigner, was closely connected with some fearful act or desire that had been successfully perpetrated in the earlier part of his life. Of this fact, such portions of his intercourse with those persons as have been already developed to the reader, furnish repeated and convincing testimonials. It may, therefore, be readily conjectured what course he had resolved upon pursuing in this dangerous emergency. It was a struggle in which life was concerned, and in which life might be forfeited; and it cannot be reasonably supposed that he whose profligate youth had wantonly sacrificed the happiness of a friend to his licentiousness and curiosity, and even now awaited the accomplishment of a scheme still more dark and atrocious, would hesitate to adopt any means, however criminal, which seemed likely to ensure his safety. It has been seen how artfully he avoided the melancholy spectacle which his villany had brought about; and it must have been observed that this disposition, which might in some cases be ascribed to a latent sense of shame and remorse, was, in his, the natural effect of a cause distantly removed from both.

At sundown the housekeeper, bent upon fulfilling her threats, departed from the house. He noted her from his chamber as she unbolted and closed behind her the ponderous gate; and immediately seizing a glittering poniard, which lay all unsheathed upon his table, and which he took the precaution to return to its case or scabbard, concealed the weapon in his vest, and stole out of the mansion by a secret passage which we have already taken occasion to describe. Effectually screened from her sight by the thick bushes and trees with which the road was lined on either side, he tracked the old crone to the Three Black Crows, where, still unobserved, he overheard her say to the worthy superintendent of that establishment, who sat, according to custom, in front of his door, that she intended to sup with him that evening. This communication was, as might be expected, succeeded by several questions from the loquacious personage alluded to, touching her whereabouts and designs, which the beldame's habitual taciturnity abruptly repelled. Rosalind did not abide the remainder of their colloquy, which, he felt convinced, would shortly be terminated, but directing his steps to the Old Sanctuary, where he expected she would pass in the progress of her journey that night, was soon involved in the close thicket which encircled its crumbling ruins. Here we leave him for the present, and return to Mr. Merrygold and his adopted daughter.

Upon ascertaining the particulars of his story from the messenger, he buttoned up his coat, sunk his broad brimmed white hat deeper upon his brow, and grasping the ivory head of his old-fashioned cane in the palm of his hand, while he brought the cane itself smartly to the ground, declared his intention not to eat, drink, or sleep until his favourite, Ned, should be found. He only delayed a minute to comfort little Nora, who appeared much more aggrieved than a child would naturally be supposed to be under like circumstances, and to give some necessary directions to the servant; then mounting his grey pony, which was in readiness for its rider at the door, immediately spurred the animal into a gallop. As he turned up a long avenue leading to the main road, and was thus entirely hidden from the maiden's eye, her fears, which had been temporarily allayed by his assurances of success, were revived in all their overwhelming painfulness and strength. A thousand extravagant causes were assigned for the youth's absence, by her young fancy, which a more matured or enlightened mind would have readily rejected as obscure and improbable, but which, nevertheless, influenced her judgment and depressed her spirits. Not the least of these ungrounded apprehensions were the mystic tales she had frequently heard, concerning the Old Sanctuary, and the nocturnal orgies of its grisly visitants. It is not easy to conceive the state of mental disquietude and perplexity to which the poor child was reduced by these chimerical notions. Unable, in her artlessness and innocence, to comprehend the thrilling interest which she experienced in Edward St. Julian's fortunes, she had sensibly nurtured a secret passion for the youth which now became a prolific subject of uneasiness and alarm. This will the more readily appear, when it is remembered that he was among the first to exhibit any solicitude in her welfare when she resided with the schoolmaster.   It may be added, too, that the extreme comeliness of his person had no tendency to mar the impression produced by his kindness, which, together, gradually concentrated the dawning light of her affections, and woke into being a passion that is seldom known at so early a period of life.

In the agitation of her feelings, little Nora sought the solitude of her chamber, and strove to solace herself with hopes of Mr. Merrygold's success, and the young man's safety; but her fears, and an excited fancy, almost maddened her brain, by appalling pictures of the mysterious shrine, to which, despite the most serious efforts, her mind still wildly reverted.   The faint glimmerings of twilight had been long superseded by the sable majesty of night.   The hour of sleep had come and past—and she still continued her weary vigil, all alone in the modest chamber which had been appropriated to her use by the naturalist.   To a harrowed mind, the objects by which it happens to be surrounded, are, generally speaking, either a source of comfort, or additional care.   Upon the scanty furniture of the apartment, her eyes wandered from time to time, scanning them with vague apprehensions as they were alternately invested by her morbid conceptions with dismal hues and unshapely forms.   Seven!—eight!—nine!—ten!—had successfully vibrated in her ears, and their dizzy echoes thrilled the awful stillness around like the monotonous chime of distant bells.   The flickering taper whose dim light illuminated her chamber was nearly spent, and at dreary intervals shed a quivering radiance on that figured arras that decorated the walls ; thus, imparting to its motley groups of grotesque figures an appearance of motion which made her heart's pulse beat with redoubled violence.   In vain she turned from this sight, and endeavoured to fasten her attention on a diminutive couch, which stood within a few steps of the spot that she herself occupied. There again new subjects of terror awaited her : for the refreshing wind which now and then cooled her heated temples, or detached the dew drops of perspiration which hung, like beads, around her brow, by turns blew apart, and again united, its thin white curtains, as the outstretched arms with which unearthly spirits are supposed to embrace their victims. She started up, pallid and trembling, from her seat, and mechanically sought the window.   Not a solitary star twinkled in the broad expanse above, and thick volumes of grey clouds, through which the moon was barely revealed, were alone discernible as they rolled in fantastic wreaths along the sky.   Ever and anon, the shrill wind might be heard whistling through the forest, whose tall pines, with their creaking branchlets, swung to and fro, or bent their shaggy heads before the heralds of the approaching storm ; while, like a troubled sea, the dark mass of foliage below heaved and howled as if in defiance of its power.   A few straggling oaks, standing in stern array upon the outskirts of the wood, presented an unbending front to each sweeping blast, and, as stalwart champions preparing for the strife, hoarsely murmured their instructions to the woodland host.

" Where—where could Edward be in such a night ?" the child mentally ejaculated, and the wildest conjectures again whispered their gloomy responses to the inquiry. " Others—to whom he had been less kind, who had less cause to be grateful—others were on foot, in this frantic shock of the elements, seeking for the lost youth.   Why should she shrink, why hesitate to follow their example ?"   In an instant her mind was resolved. " She would expose herself to the coming tempest, and, braving its fury, thread the winding forest in his search.   She would seek for him on the blasted heath, or the furrowless meadow, or the leaf-strewn banks of the boiling stream.   She would meet—she would save—or perhaps she would die with him !"

With swelling heart and throbbing brain the orphan girl now rushed out of her chamber, and, swiftly ascending the staircase, abandoned the dwelling.   Traversing a spacious

THE CONFLAGRATION IN THE FOREST.

[With crackling sound, the spreading blaze, swayed to and fro by the atmospheric strife, divided itself into thin streaks, which, like serpents, enwreathed themselves swiftly around each other.]

common which was spread out before it, she speedily reached the neighbouring wood, and, notwithstanding a thousand voices of admonishment rang in her ears, continued her fruitless search in its complicated mazes. Now she passed under huge trees—then she forced her way through entangled growths of shrubbery—then again the heather grass moistened her feet. The wild partridge darted up with rustling noise before her; but she marked it not. At length, the old ruins, peering darkly above their close cincture of shivering underwood, stood in her path. Thrusting aside, or trampling down, the opposing pine saplings and luxuriant weeds which composed the latter, she was fast winning her way to the sanctuary, when a piercing shriek attracted her attention. At once she darted into a by-path from whence it seemed to proceed, imagining, in the delirium of her thoughts, that it might be *he*. She had scarce time to behold the figure of a man bending over a body, which lay at her feet, when she felt the grasp of an iron hand upon her, and a glittering object flitted across her vision. At this moment, the moon, struggling forth from a dense mass of clouds, shed a passing lustre on her countenance, which was turned heavenward by the backward inclination of her frame.

" Gods !" exclaimed the ruffian, apparently recognising her lineaments by the uncertain light, "what have I done? Thank the moon," he added; "it has saved your life;" and, dropping the uplifted steel, he released his hold upon the maiden, who, exhausted by the fatigues she had undergone, and the terror which her situation inspired, fell senseless, with a faint cry, athwart the prostrate form.

He cast a hasty glance upon his former victim, whispering to himself, " So, braggart, thy prating is for ever silenced !" then, thrusting aside the protruding foliage of the adjacent copse, was about to retreat from the scene of his guilt, when a transient beam from on high again faintly illumined the deep obscurity around. It shone full upon his face, and, for a short time, the features of Philip Rosalind were distinctly discernible.

CHAPTER XV.

No! not the dog, that watched my household hearth,
Escaped.   *   *   *   *   *
All perished !—I alone am left on earth !
To whom nor relative nor blood remains ;
No! not a kindred drop that runs in human veins !—*Gertrude of Wyoming*.

—— Now open wide, my sire, thy grave ;
Thy curse hath dug it deeper for thy son.
*   *   *   The race of Siegendorf is past.—*Werner*.

WHILE the events narrated in the last chapter were transpiring in the forest, a far different, but equally melancholy scene, was observable in St. Julian mansion. Alone, in his chamber, sat its grief-stricken owner, brooding over the probable fate of a son in whom his seared and bleeding heart had finally concentred all its shattered affections. His two hands, which rested upon his knees, served, in some measure, to support his weakened frame, which was bent forward low, in the sullen posture of comfortless dejection, while his drooping head, deeply sunk between his shoulders, sought a shelter in his breast, and thus concealed the haggard lineaments of his face from observation. In this sorrowful attitude he had continued since the morning, at which period the intelligence of his son's disappearance reached him, refusing all consolation whatever, and obstinately denying himself the common aliments of life.

"No," he replied to the aged butler, who, after having exhausted the forenoon in fruitless researches for his young master, would have urged upon him a little wholesome food, and, with that view, took the liberty of expatiating on the danger of persisting in such a course,—"no, old man,—no! Food is for the hungry; take it to the hungry; I am not of them. Yes!" he added, wildly, a short time after, seeming totally to forget the butler's presence, and following the bent of his gloomy reflections,—"I said it—I knew it—a higher power declared to me it was the last time I should embrace thee, my poor boy. Oh! it is hard to be thus despoiled of all the treasures of existence;—one by one to have them wrenched from our determined grasp;—hopes blighted in the bud— the lovely wasting in their beauty—the strong cut down in their strength—branch after branch torn rudely off from the parent tree, till its blasted trunk is left rotting, deserted, in the sand;—but I murmur not, for it is the harvest my own folly sowed, whose bitter fruits I reap; and thy will, oh, Lord, is the will of thy servant." The last few words were spoken in a very subdued tone of voice, and, as if recollecting himself, he gazed stedfastly on the trusty domestic, whom he had forgotten, in the agitation of his mind, to dismiss, and calmly continued:—"You see, I lack not food. Search out the needy; bread is for the needy—for the beggar on the road-side, not the beggar of the heart, who has lost his precious wealth of joys that never can return again."

It was now midnight, and the tempest raged with unmitigated violence without. Not a single light illumined the apartment, and, save a few broken moonbeams which, at long and dreary intervals, suddenly came and went, shedding a transient and confused radiance into the chamber, the objects around were entirely invisible.

"At this hour," exclaimed the aged sire, who, as we have already seen, laboured under a species of religious delusion, which led him to mistake every veering impulse of his unsettled will for a revelation of Providence,—"at this hour we parted yesternight—at this hour must I go forth to seek him. The home of Philip Rosalind shall this night echo to the tread of an injured man. I will rouse him from his slumbers—if, indeed, the wicked be permitted to sleep—and ask him for my child. Yes, Almighty Father! methinks I see thy finger on his walls, even as it gleamed, with burning signs, upon Belshazzar; and, behold! I hasten to do thy bidding!"

Rising precipitately from his seat, he staggered out of his chamber, and groping through several dark and intervening passages, betook himself to a winding flight of steps, which conducted to a spacious apartment below. Here he paused for a while in order to recover his strength, which had been entirely exhausted by his recent efforts, and, in a tone which grew gradually fainter and fainter, as he spoke, called upon the ancient domestic to awake and assist him. No voice responded to the summons, save those of the hollow echoes which his own disturbed. "He, too," he mournfully added, "has deserted me; he, too, is gone. Thou didst predict it, my father, and thy prophecy will soon be verified: already is the home of my ancestors desolate." The furious winds drowned his groans of lamentation, as they swept howling by, and the watch-dog's distant bark, from the neighbouring plantations, dwelt in prolonged and discordant notes upon his ear. He feebly tottered to another part of the hall, where, with the assistance of flint and steel, he soon kindled a torch, that lay apparently in readiness for use, at the foot of the staircase; then, raising it on high, sallied forth, by the light of a sickly glare, which it shed upon the naked walls, into the open air. Here the obscurity was awfully profound. The faint moonbeams, which a few minutes before threw a pallid and uncertain lustre on the scene, were now intercepted by vast mountains of dense black clouds, which entirely overspread the horizon. Nothing could be distinguished beyond such objects as the streaming torchlight momentarily glanced upon in shivered and scattering lines, as the aged wanderer advanced with faltering steps upon his journey. " The wind blows very bleak," he muttered, shivering like an aspen in every limb, and crossing his arms upon his breast; " but what boots it? I can endure the cold for *thee*, my lost, my only child!" Thus incoherently whispering his passing thoughts, he struggled against the depressing weakness that weighed down his frame, and staggered on towards the forest. He speedily found himself involved in a long avenue, intercepted by numerous cross paths, which led into the deepest recesses of the wood, and which constantly bewildered, by diverting his attention from the main road. A deafening din, not unlike the fearful clash of contending armies, thundered without intermission around him, and might well have alarmed any mind less agitated than his own. But the inner conflict of his feelings left no room for those disquieting apprehensions which the physical commotion was so well calculated to arouse. While in the act of crossing one of the narrow ways, or passages, alluded to, a dreadful oath, accompanied by the most blasphemous imprecations on the storm, caused him to turn towards the quarter from whence they seemed to arise, when the dim torch-light discovered to his view something resembling a male form, within two yards from the spot on which he stood. Almost immediately the lambent flame again stretched out towards the strange figure, and waved its trembling light about his head.

" Philip Rosalind!" ejaculated the old man, shrinking suddenly back like a shrivelled scroll, and gazing with mingled amazement and horror on the being whom he confronted.

" It is I—what then?" answered the figure, in a hoarse, guttural voice, that thrilled painfully as he spoke, and plainfully indicated the speaker's effort at assuming a degree of composure which it was impossible he should feel.

" And is it true, then, that Heaven wills it we should meet?" resumed the elder St. Julian. " I sought thy mansion but now," he continued, " that its gilded walls might look upon the abject prey of their master's machinations; nay, more, that their voices might repeat the prayers of a supplicant. A supplicant!—ay, look not on me thus—my pride vanished with my virtue—it is even so. Not in a bitter spirit, then, do I approach thee. Philip, I have abhorred thee as the friend whom thy treachery betrayed; but, as a father, I humbly implore thee now. Knowest thou aught of my lost child ?"

" Nothing," answered Rosalind, hurriedly. " Let me pass!"

" Still—still the same," said St. Julian, " a rock which no cries can move or penetrate. Pass if thou canst; a mountain of injuries defies thee to advance."

"Adrian St. Julian," said Rosalind, " thy accursed form has haunted me in dreams of the night, and visions of the day. Thoughts of thee have poisoned my blood—wrenched the wine cup from my grasp—dampened my hopes—suppressed my mirth—embittered my sorrows—plucked the smiles of cheerfulness from my cheeks, and ploughed deep and damning lines of remorse upon my brow. Mark me, I am a desperate man; stand from my path !"

" Thy path !" cried the other; " who made it thine ? Thus I hold the light; my shadow now stretches athwart the road—pass on."

" Once more I bid thee depart," said Rosalind, hoarsely.

"Not an inch will I yield, be the issue what it may!" answered the elder St. Julian, with a firmness of voice and composure of manner which left not even the shadow of a hope that his resolve might be shaken by menace or entreaty.

" Thy life, then, be the forfeit of thy obstinacy," cried the ruffian, and with these words he thrust his hand into his vest, where he expected to find his poniard; but after searching it over hurriedly to satisfy himself that it had really been lost during his hasty retreat from the Sanctuary, or dropped in the agitation of his unexpected encounter with the little girl, he stood up still and motionless as a statue, while his features, which were illumined by the new vivid glare of the torch, betrayed the varying signs of rage, confusion, and surprise.

"Lost! lost!—perdition catch the hag!" he indistinctly muttered: then suddenly rekindling, he added, "Whining dotard! again I warn thee. Back—at thy peril—back —back!"

"Never," said St. Julian, sternly.

The word was hardly spoken, when he descried, by the vacillating light of his flambeau, a spot of gore on the ruffian's habit.

"Gods!" he exclaimed in unspeakable anguish, "I see blood upon thy vest! Philip Rosalind, thou hast murdered my child!"

"Blood!" wildly echoed the wicked man, shaking from head to foot, and looking around as if the word had stirred up furies around him. "Blood!—I have no steel. Ha! ha! who says I am a murderer?"

"I!" shouted the indignant father; "I brand thee such, heartless monster. Speak it," he continued; "was it my child you butchered?"

"No—no," returned Rosalind in the same wild manner.

"Thy accents betray thee!" cried the despairing father. "Villain, finish thy work. Behold, my breast is open to the blow. Strike thy murderous blade, yet reeking with the life-blood of a son, deep into the bosom of his father!"

"Ha! ha!" laughed the ruffian, waving his hands like a madman about his head, and twisting his frame into the most hideous contortions. "Who says I did it?—the steel—the steel is gone!" and, an instant after, appearing to recall his scattered senses together, he angrily inquired, "Did I not command you to go—and—" A long gust of wind prematurely concluded the sentence.

"Go!—Philip Rosalind—go! Who shall bid the parent go, that seeks his child even in the destroyer's den? The very winds hoot at thee, wretched miscreant, and drown thy impotent clamours. Go! Where shall I go? Thou hast rifled my world of its only treasure—thou hast robbed my hearthstone of its only solace—thou hast killed my child! But mark me, remorseless assassin, thy triumph shall be short as it is ruthless. Go forth, then, and mingle with the haunts of men. Thy head shall droop before their honest glances, and the stranger's footfall in thy dwelling shall strike dismay and consternation into thy guilty heart. Yea, I tell thee, the mark of Cain is stamped indelibly on thy accursed brow. Tremble! — tremble! Friendship betrayed — affection blighted—the cries of remorse—the agonies of despair unite in mine, and send forth their voices to the Mighty Judge. Tremble! the sword of justice quivers suspended over thy head, and its unseen hand shall smite thee to the earth. Tremble, I say, for thus—thus—my fire-brand blazes buried at thy feet, as the Avenger's beacon light shall flash destruction on thy path!"

With these words, which were uttered in a stentorian voice, he lifted on high the burning staff and sunk it deep into the moistened ground. A pause, a breathless pause! like that which precedes the last struggle of the drowning wretch for life, or which coils the envenomed serpent for his deadly spring, or heralds the riving thunderbolt to its mark—such a pause ensued.

In the meantime, the flames which had curled around, and ignited the dry branches and dead foliage of some decayed saplings and noxious briars around, sped with such wonderful rapidity from object to object, that already a vast screen of flame separated the two foes.

"Thou hast charged me wrongfully," shrieked Rosalind from the other side. "I call heaven to witness, thy son—" the rest was unintelligible. With crackling sound, the spreading blaze, swayed to and fro by the atmospheric strife, divided itself into thin streaks, which like serpents enwreathed themselves swiftly around each other. Now it groaned with the rushing sound of a forger's furnace, then it widened out into one prodigious sheet of flames, displaying to the dazzled sight heaps of wiry fern and pigmy trees burnt to a vivid red, and fast crumbling into coals and ashes; then again it ascended like the fabled dragons on fiery wings to the sky, hissing as it rose, and breathing volumes of dense black smoke, dotted with innumerable sparks.

The elder St. Julian turned from the sublime but terrific spectacle which his wrath had unwittingly provoked. The parting protestations of Rosalind reached his ears, but they affected him no more than the noisy flames which rendered them indistinct. Precipitately retracing his steps, he fled with rapid strides up the dismal avenue, now brightly illuminated by the furious conflagration. He rushed recklessly through the creeping growths of underwood which grew here and there upon the heath, and which constantly obstructed his course; the heath itself was crossed, and he stood once more at the threshold of his dwelling; the last, as he deemed himself now, the last scion of his ill-fated race. Even then the unnatural strength which animated his limbs seemed unsubdued, and another effort sufficed to place him in the chamber where, fifty years before, he had seen his sire fall lifeless at his feet. But here the transient energy of his muscles gave way, and he grasped a chair on which he accidentally stumbled, and clung to it for support. Nature was overcome, and he felt that his final dissolution was at hand.

"Father—father," he cried, "I have expiated my crime—the atonement is over—thy fatal prophecy is at length fulfilled. Ye echoes of my desolate home, hearken once more to the voice whose wish ye mimicked in childhood—whose manlier strains ye loved to repeat—whose aged lamentations ye have often reverberated—whose death gasp ye soon will hear! Farewell—farewell!" His frame trembled—his grasp relaxed—he tottered and fell heavily upon the floor. Then collecting all remaining strength for the effort, he raised himself slightly up, and painfully articulated his last words. "I die forsaken and forlorn in the tenantless halls of my fathers—my Edward—Heaven—" The rest was left unspoken. Adrian St. Julian was gathered to his fathers!

CHAPTER XVI.

THE dusty old clock which ornamented the modest parlour of the Three Black Crows, had not yet told seven, when the most unusual symptoms of confusion and disorder were observable in the village. Dogs which had evacuated their mangers, and cats that had taken the same liberty with their kitchen corners, might be seen joyfully disporting themselves on the village green, while many ragged little boys and girls were endeavouring to imitate those intelligent quadrupeds to the best of their incipient ability. The pasture grounds of the vicinage appeared entirely abandoned by their numerous herds of cattle that now roamed uncontrolled, in bold defiance of all the good old rules of common law concerning brutes *damage feasant.* Crowds of people were bustling about in every possible direction, some walking and some running—some sorrowful and some smiling—some saying a good deal, and others saying nothing at all. But in the last mentioned class, who, verily, seemed to practise the philosophy of Pythagoras from intuition, we refrain, as honest chroniclers, from placing our much esteemed acquaintance, the host of the inn. He was by far too important a character to be silent at any period whatever, much less one like the present, teeming with interest and excitement. On the present occasion he had established himself upon an empty whisky cask in front of his domicile, and through the combined energies of speech, gesticulation, emphasis, and bodily contortion, sought to express his ideas of the subject which had created the excitement referred to, to a circle of gaping listeners, who were grouped in various attitudes around him. These appeared governed as to the points deserving of applause in his harangue by the ominous physiognomy of a certain wiseacre, who held a prominent position in the crowd, and whom the reader may remember to have met with in a former chapter of this work. It is, perhaps, superfluous to observe, that the innkeeper's language, at this time, was rather more elevated in respect of style, than that which he commonly employed in colloquial parlance; and consisted of disjointed scraps, which he had industriously gathered up from the hackneyed phraseology of electioneering demagogues.

"Friends and fellow citizens!" exclaimed the orator, who had now reached the middle of his discourse, "I repeat, as I repeated before, that I am sorry that there is no prospect of seeing the man that killed the woman that we saw this morning. As to the little girl—although her situation was suspicious, very suspicious, exceedingly suspicious, it is my humble opinion, nevertheless, that it isn't suspicious at all. (Approbatory nod of the wise man, and faint cheers.) When I come to consider, hem!—to consider, fellow-citizens—hem! hem!—all that I have had occasion to say, I am forced to conclude—yes! I declare it before this assembled multitude, whose fathers fought, expired, and bled for liberty, that the constitution of this widely extended country has been trampled down into the dust—I'll fight any man on this point. (Cheers—cheers.) Fellow-citizens, I feel that I am intruding upon your patience; (cries of Go on! go on!) but when . . . . amid the sands of the desert ——"

At this stage of his speech the innkeeper was interrupted by a shrill voice from within, saying,—

"Will you come and help me to pour this liquor, Mr. B., and stop making a fool of yourself? I told you those eggs would be ruined—you know it. Don't you hear me, Mr. B.? Get down from the liquor cask, and stop your nonsense!"

"Yes, my dear," answered the public speaker, in a conciliatory voice, to his spouse, and then hastened to bring his discourse to a close, something after this fashion: "Fellow citizens, as my time is too short to speak about the sands of the desert, I beg you will allow me to postpone that passage till the next election, and in the mean time, while we are waiting for the doctor so as to go on with the *post mortar* examination, I propose that we all liquor!" (Wise man rejoiced—crowd in raptures—protracted and deafening applause.)

After this eloquent peroration, the ambitious innkeeper, followed by his hearers, entered the bar-room, and proceeded to fulfil the hospitable promise which had invested the conclusion of his rhetorical effort with such thrilling interest and effect.

While in the act of doing justice to the various wines and liquors with which the innkeeper's generosity had supplied them, the attention of the mob was suddenly arrested by the appearance of a rustic vehicle in the distance, which approached at a very rapid rate, and which they hailed with the most extravagant manifestations of delight.

"Duds—it's the doctor! so it is ; I know him by his sorrel," cried one.

"Yes; that are the inderwidual.   There—you see his green specs," said another.

"By jingo ; he's a driving it for you," added a third.

Meanwhile, the conveyance speedily advanced towards its point of destination, and, in a few moments more, was reined up by the driver, with a sonorous "Gee—wo !" in front of the inn.   The country people immediately crowded around it *en masse*, as if it contained some great natural curiosity, and only gave way, when a head as round as an ordinary globe of the world, and fully equal to that familiar object in dimensions, was hastily thrust out of the coach window ; thereby exhibiting a pair of fat cheeks, inlaid with small grey eyes, which twinkled vivaciously behind a huge apparatus of green.

"There, now ; one minute, and I'm with you.   Make way in front—fine morning, thought we'd have a shower, though.   How are ye, Jenks ?—how's your wife ?—another baby will kill her, I tell you.   Is that you, Hobbs ?—taken my blue drops yet ?   That sorrel will run off if you don't stop him—hold fast—now, draw him in—so—let me out !"

These observations were made with such wonderful rapidity of utterance, by the doctor, that our manuscript has dedicated no less than three pages to their description, together with the incidental matters of blue drops and baby ; but as our limits will not permit us to quote the sagacious reflections and happy turns of speech of this venerable chronicle, we beg that our readers will exert their powers of invention in filling up the gap.

The physician of the village having fairly alighted from his coach, was soon greeted with the same unsought distinction that had been conferred upon his vehicle, and so successful was the crowd in this second attempt at stopping up the avenues of ventilation, that he is reported to have nearly died for want of space to breathe in.   We seize, therefore, on the propitious moment when he is said to have administered to farmer Jenks a punch in the abdomen, and almost simultaneously bestowed the same mark of esteem on an equally affectionate acquaintance, to draw a hasty sketch of his external peculiarities. He was a goodly lump of middle-aged mortality, rising some feet three above the ground, and so fantastically dressed withal, that one's attention could not fail to be absorbed for a moment or so by the oddity of his appearance.   His garb was composed of a short green coat fitting close to the body, and distinguished by figured horn buttons, whose sylvan devices must have appeared to a person, ignorant of his extreme fondness for the chase, rather out of character than otherwise.   A white silk vest, extending far beyond his waist, served to display a profusion of glittering chains, which were ostentatiously involved in its loopholes, and jingled melodiously at every moment of the vast rotundity which this part of his garment overspread.   Dark knee breeches, cased in top-boots, which appeared, from their enormous bulk, to be a modification of the Jack, worn by our modern militia colonels, and gentlemen of the staff, (and so fitly named after the distinguished quality of their wearers,) ended the survey, for they left no alternative, except, indeed, to view the animal inverted.   But by far the most conspicuous ornament observable in his person, and which consequently took the eye at first glance, was a huge seal appended to his fob-chain, which bore the shape of a lion's head, and was employed by the owner to give emphasis or vivacity to his language.   Such was the striking *tout ensemble* of the village doctor, as he stood surrounded by his rustic admirers on an irregular and broken pavement fronting the Three Black Crows.

"Come, masters," he cried, dealing the blows alluded to, "a little space for breathing.   The heat is intense enough, without making it hot as the *auto da fe*, which was an instrument with which good people were formerly purified for Heaven—as thou knowest, Twiddle."

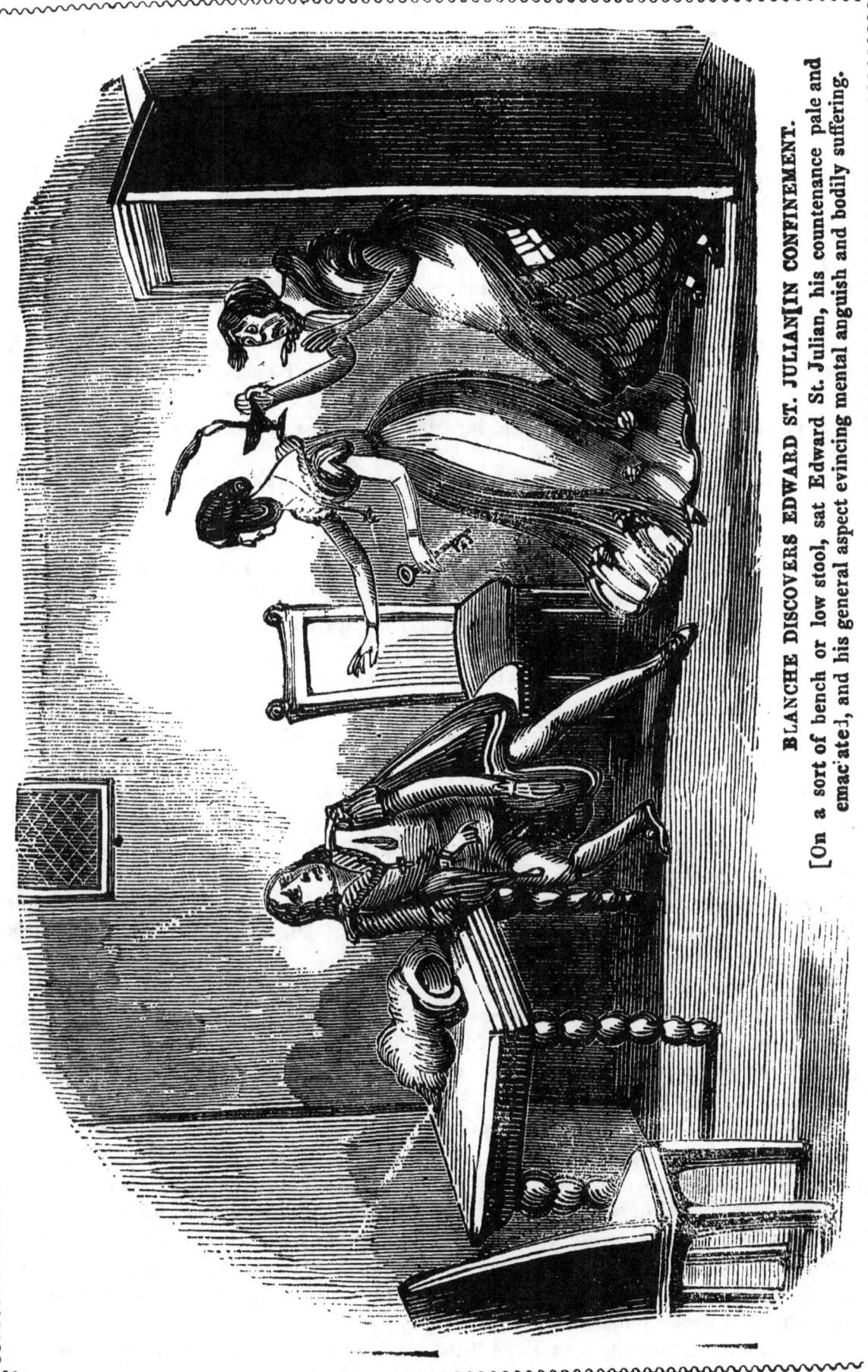

BLANCHE DISCOVERS EDWARD ST. JULIAN IN CONFINEMENT.

[On a sort of bench or low stool, sat Edward St. Julian, his countenance pale and emaciated, and his general aspect evincing mental anguish and bodily suffering.

The schoolmaster, to whom this speech was addressed, smiled with the utmost self-complacency at the implied compliment to his erudition.

"But to business, masters—to business!" continued the gentleman in green;—"*sine que non—terra est rotunda animus opibusque parati—*as Virgil hath beautifully writ in his.... hem!—(short spin of the seal)—and which means that we should suffer nothing to interfere with the calls of business;—furthermore, that of all sublunary things it is the most important, since it nourishes the animal being—(long spin)—and thus, moreover, nevertheless, notwithstanding...... hem!—(dizzy and protracted spin).... therefore, I say, let's to business. Twiddle, you are sexton, where is the corpse? Where the supposed perpetrator? Let them be shown us; we will act in our twofold capacity of physician and magistrate for the county"—(slow and dignified spin).

Mr. Twiddle looked as grave as the churchyard which it was his office to superintend, upon receiving this peremptory injunction, feeling himself deeply wounded that after a complimentary reference to his scholarship, a matter, as we have already stated, of apocryphal authority among his neighbours, that this vulgar phase of his character should be so pointedly alluded to.

He accordingly stepped forward and boldly faced the physician, while the three cornered hat trembled indignantly upon his head, and his great progenitor's shoe-buckles shone ten times brighter than before.

"Sir," he sternly commenced; "allow me to observe that I dispute your Latinity as an unnatural, unmeaning, absurd, and ungrammatical gibberish!"

"He's got his dose now, I promise you," whispered one of his enemies to a bystander.

"Undoubtedly," responded the latter.

By this time the learned disciple of Esculapius and Hippocrates had drawn himself up to his utmost height, and his seal was whizzing round with incredible velocity.

"Do you!" he replied; "'pon honour! a village clown speak of Latin to me!—*me!* Know you, sirrah, that you address a bachelor of the arts and sciences, a doctor of laws and of divinity besides, an astronomer, a metaphysician, a theologian, and, above all, an honorary member of the Edinburgh faculty of Physic. (Spin triumphant!) Give way, thou brainless neophyte in the arts and sciences. (Spin, spin, double spin.) *Sit transit gloria munde!* which if thou comprehendest not, I deign thus to promulgate in thy vernacular verbage—Stand out of the way, or, I'll kick you out of it!" (Spin protracted and overwhelming!)

Considerably softened by the *argumentum ad hominem* which his antagonist had so judiciously employed, the schoolmaster disposed himself to enter upon his official duties, and, accordingly, led the way to the Old Sanctuary, amid the universal derision of his jealous neighbours, who were delighted that his presumption had met with so decided a rebuff from the physician.

In a narrow passage, or by-way, leading to the ruins, they found the old woman's corpse, decently composed on a broad plank which was fixed transversely across several stakes and clumps of trees, and guarded by four athletic looking gentlemen, armed with hickory clubs of prodigious size, whom the classic coroner had that morning detailed to the spot; a precaution taken, as our venerable chronicle shrewdly suspects, to prevent the body from running away. A rude bench was placed on a slight eminence within two yards of the body, to which our learned justice, guided by official instinct, immediately betook himself.

At some paces from the spot stood little black-eyed Nora. She had, that morning, been discovered by a sturdy old farmer of the vicinity, lying stretched across the old woman's corpse, her garments besmeared with blood, and a dagger within an inch of her hand, which seemed to have been dropped in the morbid agitation of mind which commonly attends the perpetration of crime. She was consequently arrested upon suspicion, and being questioned as to the motives which had induced her to leave her dwelling in such a tempestuous night, coloured, faltered, and sobbed out incoherent replies, that something confirmed the horrid thoughts which had entered the minds of her captors. It was true that on the most material point she was clear as could be possibly desired; declaring her utter ignorance of the murderer, and giving such a feeble outline of his person, as her confused ideas and uncertain recollection of the event admitted; but her obstinate refusal to answer the query adverted to above, imparted a colouring of falsehood to the whole statement, which yielded at the same time a dangerous plausibility to the wildest conjectures. The maiden now reclined against the gnarled trunk of a decayed oak, of which nothing remained save the crumbling circumference, being perfectly hollow within. Her face was composed to an expression of subdued melancholy much beyond her years. As the vast assemblage approached, her glance, which had been fixed vacantly on the ground, was suddenly raised, and permitted to wander mechanically from face to face: on all of which curiosity was strongly depicted. After this casual survey, her long, silken eye-lashes fell, and their large, dreamy orbs were again cast down. A deep tinge of sadness had, indeed, crept over her features, but it served in no wise to diminish their exquisite beauty, which, like the clear blue arch above her, that the recent storm had rendered transparently bright, were still equally lovely, whether suffused with the blushes of morning, or clad in the pensiveness of eve.

The assemblage being distributed about in proper order, a sign was made by the coroner to his deputies, who then instructed the maiden to come forward and prepare herself to answer all such questions as might be proposed by their superior. She accordingly advanced, and, with a palpitating heart, paused before the judge.

"Child," quoth he, in a deep, solemn voice, "knowest thou aught of this dreadful murder?"

She trembled in every limb, and painfully faltered out a negative.

"Mark it down, Popkins," he added, addressing his clerk, a drowsy-looking youth, who sometimes acted in the capacity of postilion, and, therefore, bore about him the respective symbols of those separate dignities, having a pencil in one hand, and a horsewhip in the other—"Mark it down: she knows nought of the murder. Did you not see the murderer?" he continued.

The child nodded an assent to the question.

"Mark it down, Popkins. How now, varlet, are you asleep!" he added, giving Mr. Popkins a rap on the head, which immediately restored him to a consciousness of those important duties he had temporarily forgotten; "mark you a nod on the paper."

Against this, the scribe deferentially remonstrated, stating that a nod could not be marked upon the paper, though it might be described.

"That's because thou art ignorant of Greek, fool!" answered the coroner. "Describe me a nod, then, if thy skill goes no farther. Maiden," he continued, "thou hast equivocated—ergo, thou hast contradicted thyself—therefore—nevertheless—notwithstanding I expound it unto thee as the law of the land, that thou art committed. Officers, the prisoner is dismissed from our presence!"

These last words were spoken to the ruffians already mentioned, who removed her, not, however, without some small degree of violence, to her former station near the decayed oak.

After this summary investigation of the grounds of suspicion alleged against little black-eyed Nora, the public functionary rose slowly from his seat and proceeded to examine the corpse which lay before him. He partly withdrew the tattered cloth which covered the visage and breast, and passing his hand gently over those parts of the body, with looks of profound sagacity and some professional shakes of the head, thus addressed the twelve boors who had been appointed, as a jury, to assist him in the examination.

"Her breast," he commenced, "is very warm; and there are some, masters, the more ignorant of our profession, who would imagine, from this symptom, that she is still alive—" mutterings of astonishment throughout the multitude greeted this emphatic declaration; "but to me, these signs plainly indicate the contrary—according to that sage maxim of antiquity—*perseverando vincimus hic ejus pinto*—which means........hem! what you couldn't possibly understand, if there were words in our vulgar tongue to translate it (long and short spins alternate). *Ergo*, masters, since we have arrived at the conclusion that her soul hath departed from her body, though her body be warm, by a consideration of those internal influences which originate in objects which are the corellaries of necessary consequences, it follows, from these premises, *aut fas et nefas*, nevertheless, notwithstanding, *et cetera*, that since she is dead—she ought to be buried."

Here the speaker was interrupted by irrepressible murmurs of assent from the twelve jurors, mingled with shouts of admiration from the crowd.

"Therefore," resumed the charlatan, "in the name of this jury of twelve able-bodied men, legally impannelled, I declare the following verdict:—'Death, which, after a careful investigation of the body, we have not the slightest doubt, was produced by some natural cause or other.' Popkins, put that down, and see you mark it with two strokes underneath. Masters, the court is adjourned."

The attention of the mob was here suddenly attracted by an individual who was endeavouring to force his way through it, and appeared perfectly indifferent as to the roughness of the means which he employed to accomplish that object. Upon reaching the spot where the jurors were assembled, he looked anxiously around, and, discovering little Nora, stretched out his arms to the child, who immediately rushed towards him. The by-standers now recognised the stranger, and whispers of "Squire Merrygold!" hastily passed from mouth to mouth.

"Who dares thus violate the law of the country?" cried the magistrate, spinning his fob-seal violently, and looking daggers at the naturalist. "Knowest though not, sirrah, that thou art guilty of the heinous offence entitled a rescue?"

For a few seconds, Mr. Merrygold was unable to speak, and his lips quivered with a nervous sort of twitch, which plainly indicated that his fund of good nature and patience were entirely exhausted. At length he broke forth—"And know *you, sirrah,* why this stick was made?"

The magistrate, disdaining to articulate a negative reply, suffered his globular pericranium to perform a semi-revolution upon its axis.

"To whip thee, varlet—so it was—there! there!" and so saying, the naturalist exercised his ivory-headed cane about the sacred person of our learned justice of the quorum with so much agility and strength, that the latter, notwithstanding the encumbrance of his heavy top-boots, danced a hornpipe around the old hag's body, calling lustily the while upon his subordinates for help. These, though with apparent reluctance, finally interposed, and thus prevented their leader from being beat into a mummy.

"Let them be secured!" screamed the enraged magistrate, as soon as the intervention of his creatures ensured him against any further violence; "let them be secured, I say! Strike a functionary of the law!—a justice of the quorum! an acting magistrate of the county!—let them be secured. Take care!—Dobson! Hobbs!—let him not escape;—if he do, I hold you responsible in the name of the state. Popkins! Popkins, I say!—oh, the sluggish beast—if he were only here—to write it down in white and black that I was struck, assaulted, battered, bruised in the discharge of my official function. Treason to the state!—treason to the people!—an acting coroner battered with a stick—remember it, masters, I'll make you witnesses all—Damages!—Damages! —Damages!"

The multitude now dispersed in different directions; and while the unfortunate professional employed himself in alternately threatening his prisoners and abusing his subordinates, Mr. Twiddle, assisted by several by-standers who had lagged behind out of curiosity, proceeded to lift up the plank on which the supposed corpse was laid out, for the purpose of transporting it to the common burying-ground of the village.

CHAPTER XVII.

In darkenesse and horrible and strong prison
——————— hath sittin Palamon
Forpined, what for love and for distresse,
Who feleth double sorræ and hevinesse
But Palamon! that love distraineth so,
That wood out of his wits he goth for wo.
CHAUCER'S *Canterbury Tales.*

IT becomes necessary that the reader should here revert to the events which succeeded the arrest of the smuggler in Rosalind Mansion, and the providential escape of Blanche from a matrimonial alliance with that unprincipled voluptuary. We, therefore, abruptly take leave of the village doctor and his prisoners for the present, and shifting the incidents of our book a few pages back, return to the period in which those occurrences may be properly said to have taken place.

When the maiden recovered from the fit of unconsciousness into which her sudden and unexpected deliverance had thrown her, she eagerly inquired for her father, and requested that she might be conducted to his chamber. Thither, accordingly, attended by her private domestic, she directed her steps, trusting that his illness might fully justify the superficial account of it which the notary had given her, and secretly alarmed lest it should prove more serious than he had probably thought prudent under prevailing circumstances to reveal. Hence it may be readily imagined with what startling emotions of surprise she was visited upon entering his chamber. Every object was disposed in the nicest possible order; the bed-clothes were unruffled by a single wrinkle, the net-work or summer pavilion was still fastened within the gilded ring through which it is suffered to escape during the hours of repose; everything in the place bore an appearance which confirmed her in the thought that her father had not crossed its threshold that evening.

"It is very strange," she whispered to the servant; "and have you not seen him either?"

The girl answered in the negative ; adding that he might perhaps have gone into the library, where he sometimes went during the night.

"It may be," murmured Blanche, pausing to cast a lingering glance around the chamber, as she determined to act upon the menial's suggestion.

They now traversed with hurried steps several large apartments, pausing now and then to shield with their hands the vascillating flame of their lamp from rude gusts of wind which they occasionally encountered through an open window. Blast after blast swept wildly by without, which, joined to the deep obscurity that universally prevailed, might almost be said to invite the mind to a belief of that fantastic superstition of the North, in which the Geni of Evil, mounted on his winged steed of ghastly white, and followed by his shouting host of unearthly champions, is reported to whirl in frantic career through the aerial vault. The chambermaid, a pious Catholic girl, whose parents resided in the neighbourhood, did not fail to repeat the most lengthy invocations to the Blessed Virgin with which her memory supplied her at the time, and which were fortified by little appeals, after the manner of side speeches, to some of the sainted fathers of the Mother Church. But her mistress was agitated by fears and presentiments of a much more harassing nature. Her father's unaccountable absence wholly occupied her thoughts, and excited the most painful misgivings and conjectures.

"The saints have mercy on us ! how dark the place is !" ejaculated the maid, entering the study, and eagerly looking around for the object of their search.

"Not here !" exclaimed Blanche, despondingly, making the same observation, as she quickly succeeded her into the room.

"Father of sinners ! what have we here ?" half screamed the damsel, descrying the private door, which, it may be remembered, Rosalind had neglected to secure.

"A door !" said her mistress, in a tone which, though more subdued, was equally indicative of astonishment.

"Holy Mother, let us return, madam," suggested the affrighted domestic, trembling with terror, and averting her eye from the strange sight.

"No," said Blanche ; "I have resolved to fathom this mystery ; let us on."

The poor girl stared like an idiot into her face upon receiving this unexpected order ; this her mistress had no sooner observed than she added, gently,—

"If you fear to advance, Anna, you may return to your chamber, or remain where you now are ; I will not insist on your accompanying me in a search which may perhaps be fatal to the searcher. Providence will be my guide and protector. I have a father's safety at stake, and am therefore resolved to proceed."

"But consider, madam—consider !" remonstrated the damsel.

"I have, and my mind is resolved," interrupted her mistress ; "will you follow me or no ?"

The damsel was too well acquainted with the lofty decision of her lady's character in all matters in which duty was either really or apparently concerned, to doubt for a moment that she would fulfil the intention she had expressed ; and actuated partly by a fear to retrace her steps or remain alone in the dreary apartment in which they now stood, mingled probably with a feeling of gratitude for the many favours which Blanche had conferred upon her family and herself, consented, after a little hesitation, to follow her in the present adventure.

"I will be guide," said the young lady, seizing upon the lamp, and raising it above her head ; "it is but just that I should take the burden of danger upon myself—follow me."

So saying, they descended with some difficulty a precipitous stair, which the light revealed to view, and to which the door in question gave access. This done, they found themselves in a long gallery or aisle, paved with square granite stone, which, like the unwholesome air that circulated through the place, was damp and nauseous. The walls wore a sickly yellowish hue by the lamplight, save where the mortar appeared to have fallen off, and the dingy bricks of which they were composed were exposed to the sight. But, notwithstanding the novelty of her position, and the strange appearances around her, the young lady advanced with unfaltering steps, animated by the consciousness of duty, and sustained by that unabating confidence in the goodness of a Higher Power which we have seen was a distinguishing feature of her character. On the other hand, Anna laboured under the most depressing influences, imagining at every step some new subject of amazement and terror. They had made but little progress in the gloomy corridor, and were gliding noiselessly onward, when a deep sigh, which seemed to proceed from one of the contiguous walls, at once startled and arrested them both. Anna dropped upon her knees, and raising her hands devoutly upwards, called aloud for the whole fraternity of saints to assist her.

"Who is there?" inquired Blanche, in a firm voice, though her heart palpitated audibly, and the extreme pallor of her cheeks belied the affected composure of her manner.

"You should know me," briefly answered a hollow, but still familiar voice, and again a fearful stillness reigned throughout the place.

"Edward St. Julian!" faintly articulated the young lady, resting against the opposite wall for support. "Good Heavens! what can this mean?" The light now shone upon what appeared to be a massive door, secured by various bars and cross bolts, besides a ponderous and rusty lock. A key of corresponding dimensions was suspended on the wall, and obviously intended to give admittance to the dungeon.

"Assist me, Anna," said the maiden, striving to control her sudden agitation, "assist me, for I feel a strange weakness creeping over my frame, and my strength seems all expended!" And, assisted by the trembling domestic, she sought to unfasten the long iron bars which intersected the singular portal. These yielded one by one to their united exertions, and, in an instant more, the dusty lock harshly groaned as it reluctantly turned under the key, and the unwieldly door itself swung back ajar upon its screaming hinges. A chilling current of air rushed out of the dungeon, which would have extinguished their lamp, had not Blanche promptly screened its streaming flame with her gown and hands. It soon abated, and she entered the subterranean chamber, followed by her domestic. But here a scene more astonishing and painful than those which, in such wonderful succession, had preceded it, presented itself to their view. On a sort of bench or low stool, sat Edward St. Julian, his countenance pale and emaciated, and his general aspect strongly evincing the combined effects of mental anguish and bodily suffering. Around him a few ordinary chairs, encrusted with dust, were promiscuously scattered here and there, which, with a table, whose material and construction betokened it of a much more respectable derivation and breeding, constituted all the furniture of the uncouth apartment. The apartment itself was diminutive, and, as we had occasion before to observe, received its scanty supply of light from a small grated window, so much elevated above the ground, that it was utterly impossible to reach it without a ladder, and which seemed designed to aggravate the torments of those who should be there confined, by elating their minds with delusive hopes of escape and liberation, that it might baffle their exertions made to realize them.

The young man glanced sadly upwards as Blanche entered, accompanied by the trembling damsel, who was not yet quite sure whether the object she beheld was a devil, a witch, or a man, and who was diligently sketching airy crosses in every possible direction, with the tip end of her finger, to keep off the little imps or subordinate devils, that might be supposed to swarm about the chamber.

"And is it you, then, madam, that are my gaoler?" he asked, in a proud but trembling voice.

"Your gaoler, Edward?" echoed the half bewildered maiden, who could not but feel as much softened as surprised by the melancholy situation of her lover. "For Heaven's sake, speak not thus wildly!"

"Who led you to this spot?" he continued, interrupting her.

"The veriest accident," she answered, looking around as she spoke; "I sought my father, who was reported ill, and chancing on a secret aperture in his study, wandered hither in quest of him."

"Is it so?" said Edward, fixing his piercing eyes inquiringly upon her, as if he half mistrusted what she had spoken.

The young lady drew herself up with that imposing stateliness of movement which nothing but offended dignity ever prompts, and superior loveliness can so well execute; while a rich crimson mantled on her fair cheeks, which might have been mistaken for the beautiful confusion which delicately tinges the virgin's first confession of love, had not the fire that flashed indignantly from her eyes declared it the tacit rebuke of insulted pride.

"It were as unbecoming, sir, for me to answer such a question, as it was unmannerly in you to propound it," the lady calmly replied.

"Forgive me, Blanche," the youth cried, with enthusiasm; but here he abruptly paused, and coldly added, "madam! you see my mind wanders, since I can forget even your new estate." The maiden did not speak, and he resumed:—"Believe me, I meant not to wound you when I spoke. A miserable wretch, whom fortune and your contumely have alike singled out for their victim, may well be forgiven if, in the bitterness of his anguish, he unwittingly offend what most he cherishes upon earth. Blanche——"

The pathos of his manner, no less than his emaciated aspect, deeply moved the maiden's heart, and she averted her head, that the unbidden tear, which glistened in her eyes, might escape his observation. He marked the movement, and ascribing it to a far different motive, immediately checked himself, and added:—

"Miss Rosalind, it may be that I am free with your name,—too free for one who, whatever he may have been, is now a stranger! But the associations which your presence awakes, like magic, into life, are so bright, so beautiful, so dear, that the present is insensibly forgotten in the past, and I bethink me only of the blithesome days when I loved, and fondly dreamed that I was loved again. It is past, you would say? True! with you it has, doubtless, ere this, been consigned to oblivion; but to me, the memory of that blighted affection—that crushed, faded, worthless flower I so carefully tended when its spring-tide freshness could repay me for my toil—that relic of the sweet delusion in which I thought myself secured beyond suspicion, blessed beyond deserving,—is, to my seared heart, trifling as it may seem, a treasure which none may justly estimate who have never been smiled upon, and then—then—cruelly forgotten, like me!" He paused an instant, but her face still continued averted from his glance, and he continued:—"Here, in this loathsome dungeon, where the hand of villany has placed me—villany which I trace not to its source, for that I would spare you a pang on my account—even here, half frantic with thoughts of my wrongs, half exhausted with the cravings of hunger——"

TWITTER'S TERROR AT THE RESUSCITATION OF THE SUPPOSED CORPSE.

[The old woman finally hazarded a desperate exertion, which placed her in a sitting posture on the bier. She then feebly beckoned the schoolmaster to advance.]

" Hunger !" interrupted the maiden, dwelling with manifest anxiety upon his haggard features.

" I pray for death to release me from a life which could never be shared with her who, but yesterday, was my own—my affianced wife, and is now the bride of another. Blanche Rosalind, it was madness to think of that ! But still, for all that, as for all, I forgave— I blest you !"

" Edward !" the young lady sobbed aloud, unable longer to repress her emotions, " I have deeply wronged you, it is true ; but in one thing have I been blameless and faithful. My heart is free ! In the present, as in the past, I am thine—thine alone—thine for ever !"

These words had scarce escaped her lips, when she was ardently clasped in the arms of the devoted youth, who forgot all the sufferings he had undergone in this single moment of unspeakable rapture and felicity.

The blushing maiden immediately disengaged himself from his embrace, and, remarking that she would not press him to give an account of the strange disaster which had befallen him until he should have partaken of some strengthening food, beckoned Anna, who had, by this time, fully recovered from her fright, to advance with the light into the corridor.

They briskly retraced the path, and soon arrived at the elegant dining apartment of the mansion. Here the domestic promptly served up an ample meal of cold meats and fruit, to which Edward is reported, by our minute and truthful chronicle, to have done the utmost justice. He could not avoid observing, however, that Blanche had undergone a sudden and material change in their passage to this apartment ; for which he found it impossible to account, having forgotten, in the blissful emotions which had been recently awakened in his mind, and the subjects of distraction afforded by the knife and fork, what she had communicated to him concerning her father.

The young lady secretly reproached herself for having permitted her affection for the youth even a momentary triumph over her filial concern and solicitude. Hence an expression of deep melancholy overspread her downcast features, as, with eyes bent upon the ground, and hands carelessly folded, she pondered over the mysterious occurrences which had so recently transpired, and of which her parent's sudden absence was the first.

The youth had no sooner appeased the more urgent cravings of his appetite, than he rose from the table, and, taking a seat beside her, hastened to recite the brief narrative of his capture and imprisonment in the subterranean cell.

" My dear Blanche," he continued, taking her hand, which was not withdrawn, " you are doubtless curious to be apprised by what extraordinary vicissitude of fate I was incarcerated in the gloomy prison to which Providence conducted your steps. This may be briefly told. Upon leaving you in the arbour last evening, I had proceeded but a short distance on my way, when two ruffians, disguised as maskers, unexpectedly started up behind me, who immediately secured my person and blindfolded my eyes. After being paraded through all the secret windings of the forest, I was finally confined in the dismal abode where you accidentally discovered me. What their motives may have been I know not ; certes, they were vile cowards—Blanche, are you ill ?" he inquired, interrupting himself, and gazing intently on the maiden, who had grown agitated and pale.

" No," she replied, making a visible effort to subdue her feelings ; " go on."

" I say, they were vile cowards," he continued, " to deny me my freedom, when I offered to make it good by opposing them both, unarmed and friendless as I was. But— be it so ! Their day shall come ; for, if my vengeance overtake them not, that of a higher Power will! One of these cut-throats spoke Italian; I heard him mutter a few words as he closed the door of my cell, which extinguished his lantern; and the other—Blanche! Good Heavens! you shake like an aspen in the breeze——"

" No, no," quickly returned the young lady, " I tremble not; but the remembrance of that dreary place, now that I am out of it, appals me. Besides, my father's singular absence distresses my mind—indeed, you said true—I am unwell." She rose from her seat, and, after a short pause, added—" Anna will show you to an apartment at the other extremity of the building, where you may rest for the night without fear of interruption, and depart unobserved in the morning. Nay, you must stay; the tempest is too violent without—good night!"

She tendered her hand to the youth as she spoke, who raised it respectfully to his lips, and, after some brief instructions to her servant, abruptly retired to her chamber, where harassing conjectures and distracting dreams conspired with the raging storm to keep her awake during the remainder of the night.

In the meantime Edward St. Julian was conducted by Anna to a small, but commodious chamber, situated in the southern extremity, or wing, of the building, and which gave access through a private door to the elegant gardens around it. He now dismissed the damsel, and with little difficulty succeeded in composing himself to slumbers, which, though profound, were constantly broken and interrupted by the loud clamour of the warring elements.

It was near morning when an unequal and heavy tread in the passage-way, leading to his dormitory, suddenly awakened him from his sleep. He crept noiselessly from his bed, and, placing his ear to the door, heard the following incoherent sentences spoken in a voice which he at once recognised for that of Rosalind—" His words ring in my ears—Oh! the torments of my soul—who says—*I did it*—ha! ha!......Gods! what an—echo—this cursed place—hath!" He could hear no more. Throwing open the private door alluded to, the young man hastily traversed the garden walk, and directed his steps towards his own mansion.

CHAPTER XVIII.

Upon reaching his mansion, Edward St. Julian hurriedly ascended the winding stair which conducted to his father's chamber, and, agitated by a secret consciousness of impending evil, eagerly rushed into the apartment. In doing so, he stumbled upon an obstacle which obstructed his way, and, glancing downwards, beheld the lifeless form of his departed sire at his feet. It were difficult to describe the feelings of horror which this terrible spectacle excited in his mind. There lay the old man, stretched at full length upon the floor—his features colourless and wan, but still retaining the expression of mingled sorrow and serenity which had ushered his soul into eternity. He knelt beside the corpse—he parted its thin white locks, and touched the high, expansive brow which bore, even in death, the impress of the heroic mind that, in life, had sheltered there; it was chilly, bloodless, and stiff.—" Oh, God!" he mentally exclaimed, involuntarily recoiling as he gazed—" this, then, is death!" The whole truth flashed on his bewildered brain. He had deemed the captive one—lost; he had perished forsaken and forlorn—abandoned by all—without friends, without kindred, without a word of hope—a tear of regret, a comfortless, broken-hearted man! The fatal prediction was, then, literally fulfilled! But his oath of vengeance on the ruthless destroyer of his race, should that, too, perish?—should that, too, be forgotten?   No! the grave gave forth its hollow accents—*No!* The spirits of his fathers started up in crepuscular dimness around him, and a trumpet blast pealed it—No! He pressed the dead man's icy hand within his own, and muttered his prophetic words as he rose—" Vengeance may be tardy, but it is certain!"   *   *   *   *   *   *

An hour passed—and Rosalind was seated alone in his chamber. He had that morning heard of the Italian's arrest, and bent upon saving himself from exposure, had instructed his servants to report that he was on the road to Charlestown, while he made diligent preparations for immediate departure. But these plans were suddenly changed by the arrival of a secret messenger from his confederate, who sincerely promised, whatever might befall, not to betray him, and, moreover, assured him that he had discovered certain means of escape. This intelligence had partially restored the wonted composure of his mind and manner, when a domestic hastily entered the apartment and presented him with a scroll of paper, which he said had been left by Edward St. Julian.

"Edward St. Julian!" exclaimed Rosalind, and his eyes turned with a sort of wild instinct to the secret door. It was open, and until then he had not observed it. His fingers now mechanically unfolded the paper, and he read as follows :—

" I could deliver you into the hands of public justice—but I forbear." He breathed more freely. " Adrian St. Julian is no more, but his avenger lives. We must meet.— Flight were futile : henceforth, I am your shadow !"

"Thou liest!" cried Rosalind, dropping the paper, and dwelling with frantic looks upon his own shadow, which slightly moved upon the wall as he made an ineffectual effort at flight in the sudden delirium of his guilty mind. " Minion ! would you have me butchered ?" he cried out to his servant, as he pointed to the unsubstantial mockery before him. " Seize him!—there—there- -the ——" The words died away in his throat, and he sank, overpowered by the weight of his own thoughts, into the arms of his attendant.

CHAPTER XIX.

SINCE his unexpected encounter with the spirits of the wood, Mr. Twiddle's aversion for supernatural appearances, which, owing to the nervous susceptibility of his temperament, was naturally intense enough to render him often uneasy, had gradually assumed the fearful form of a morbid affection or constitutional disease. He now retired to his chamber long before the sun was fairly down, and disdained to be thereto illuminated, as of yore, by

> "The glimmerings of a waxen flame."

S: c . the awful scene which had rendered him so irreconcilably averse to his office, he had never been troubled to discharge any of its important duties, and now that the critical moment arrived in which one of its most appalling responsibilities must necessarily be attended to, he trembled and shrunk with secret dread at the uncomfortable prospect. Besides, there was one trivial circumstance involved in the present case, from which he shrewdly augured the most unhappy results. The two men who assisted him on the present occasion to convey the body of the old woman to the village churchyard, had long been reputed among the bitterest of his foes, and he concluded from the readiness with which they had come to his aid, that they were bent on the accomplishment of some sinister object in regard to himself.

Having reached the antique porch, they entered the church, and proceeded to deposit

their unconscious burden in the aisle.   The schoolmaster had overheard frequent whis-
perings between his two assistants while on the road, and the unpleasant suspicions to
which they had given rise in his mind were now fully confirmed by the eccentric manner
in which they demeaned themselves towards him.

"Now, we'll fix him," said the learned boor (for he was one of these amiable personages), apart to his companion.

"Ondoubtedly," responded the other, who never failed to employ this emphatic part
of speech whenever an opportunity presented itself.

"Twiddle," resumed the first, again addressing the schoolmaster, "the boys have been
thinking lately as how you have no more *reel grit* than a dead goose ; and, as I'm a friend
of yourn, and always was, I'm of opinion that you ought to be put to the *ordeel* now, as
parson Smith calls it."

Mr. Twiddle's countenance exhibited all the hues of the rainbow during this brief
discourse, and he had already opened his lips to remonstrate against the anticipated
violence, when his invidious neighbour continued :—

"You needn't argify against it—no! not a bit.   You might as well try to skin a crab.
We intend to shut you up in this here place for a spell or so—and now you've got it
straight."

"Shut me up here!" quoth the pedagogue, chattering with fear.

"Ah! ay! and here goes for it!" And the mischievous rustic advanced towards the
door, followed by his accomplice, and shaking the keys, which he had been careful to
secure upon his entrance into the building, around the end of his fore-finger.

"Good friends—kind friends!" expostulated the affrighted wight; "anything else but
that!   For mercy's sake—for pity's sake!"

"Ha! ha!" shouted the boors, in whom his alarm, instead of awakening compassion,
excited the most unbounded merriment.

"You'll argue with me again about the pope, Mr. Scholard," cried the important man,
triumphantly, as he reached the door and hastily forced the key into the lock; "you will,
eh! I've got the keys of St. Peter this time, and I'll make you sweat for cursing at a
man of my standing in dog Latin !"

And with a rude laugh they quitted the church and turned the key in the lock.

In this dilemma, the schoolmaster sought to solace his fears by the hope that they
would release him from his confinement before nightfall, until which time he deemed
himself amply protected by the daylight from any and every species of supernatural
annoyance.   Under the cheering impression of this unwarranted conjecture he entered
the prim Miss Chinchilly's pew, expecting to glean at least as much information from
the books of that rigid devotee, as he had had the good fortune to derive from those of
her friends and rivals.   But, in this, he was signally disappointed; for she had taken
the wise precaution to conceal all her works on devotion, and the curious scraps, which
they, also, probably contained, in a small drawer attached to the seat which she usually
occupied.   This formidable obstacle, however, did not totally daunt our enterprising
sexton, who immediately drew from his vest pocket a huge bundle of keys, which he
was patient enough to apply, one after the other, to the lock, till an appropriate substi-
tute for the original was obtained.   At this moment a strange and unaccountable sound
fell upon his ear.   It was a low groan like that of a person striving to make some painful
effort, and, besides the paralyzing shock which it gave to the schoolmaster's senses,
awakened the darkest images in his imagination.   He turned with the celerity of a spin-
ning-top upon the high heels which were generally used as a pivot to his frame, and

facing the supposed corpse, beheld a thin and shrivelled hand projecting from the tattered sheets in which it was thickly enveloped. Not more intensely appalling to the murderous Spilatro was the bloody vision that he suddenly witnessed, amid the fetid exhalations and mysterious glooms of the Inquisition, than this unnatural sight appeared to our luckless hero, who, with jaws distended, and eyeballs wildly starting from their expanded sockets, gazed panic stricken upon it.

Presently the stiffened fingers slightly moved, and a faint voice cried,—

" Help !—help !"

" Oh ! most ethereal fairy !" bellowed the schoolmaster, despairingly, making a deep genuflection as he spoke—" pardon me—in pity, pardon me, and never more shall I commit a similar offence ! never wilfully open a drawer without the rightful owner's permission, nor use my keys for other purposes than those for which the manufacturer intended them."

"Come !— come !" repeated the strange voice, in a somewhat louder tone than before.

He raised his folded arms imploringly as he concluded this humiliating supplication, and looked in hopeless despair, towards the beldame's body.

The old woman, who, though severely wounded in the forest, had not been quite killed, and who was, since then, merely sunk into a sort of lethargic sleep or stupor consequent upon the copious effusion of blood which had flowed from the deep gash made by Rosalind in her left side, now began to recover her senses gradually, and finally hazarded a desperate exertion, which placed her in a sitting posture on the bier. She then feebly beckoned the schoolmaster to advance.

" I am awake—alive—near—near !" breathed out the old woman with obvious difficulty and pain—" fear not ——"

Thus encouraged, the schoolmaster was finally persuaded to approach, and assist her with his arm, though it was obvious that he did so with extreme reluctance. To her inquiries respecting the events of the morning, he replied by a succinct and particular account of all the circumstances which had transpired that morning ; and he could not fail to observe during this minute narration, that her countenance grew alternately grave and gay, though the latter seemed at best but the reflection of anxious and gloomy thoughts. He dwelt at length on the most prominent features of his subject, and was proceeding to expatiate on some of its more subordinate relations, when the old crone interrupted him with a request that she should be secretly transported to his dwelling, and there concealed till the restoration of her health.

" What, gull the people into thinking that you are defunct, when you are only debilitated !" exclaimed the sexton, in an indignant tone, " no, faith, not I ! No, dame— no. Trust me, I know my duties as a Christian, a member of society, and, above all, a beadle of the county, better than to have any share or concern in your people who die without the aid of a physician, and return to life just as mysteriously as they appeared to go out of it."

The old woman made no reply to this lengthy harangue, but, thrusting her emaciated hand into a bag which she had hidden among the tattered rags that composed her garment, drew forth several pieces of gold, and presented them to the speaker. The sexton's eyes glistened much brighter than his grandfather's shoe-buckles had ever shone, albeit they had been subjected to the salutary influence of friction for a century and a half past. He gazed upon the pieces with looks of unfeigned astonishment, and, without waiting to satisfy his curiosity or his conscience as to the means and manner by which they had been obtained, somewhat abruptly conducted them to their ultimate destination—his pocket.

The two rustics returned at the expiration of an hour, and were exceedingly disappointed and surprised on finding that the schoolmaster had located himself immediately beside the corpse, and was apparently quite unconcerned about the dangerous propinquity.

They sulkily returned him the keys, and, after expressing a hope that their little "bit of fun" had not materially interfered with or retarded his professional duties, departed like men who have wasted their time and ingenuity in annoying another, and are themselves eventually discomfited for their pains.

CHAPTER XX.

An unusually damp and misty morning ushered in the eventful day which had been set apart for the trial of little Nora. A dense and almost impenetrable vapour clothed the western shores of the Ashley, rendering its dark line of shaggy woodlands barely discernible, whose dismal hues were now dimly blended with the louring and unfriendly skies above it. A dull, leaden hue tinged the troubled waters of the river; and its boisterous waves, like wild and untamed steeds, rushed recklessly onward in the full career of unbridled impetuosity. At this early hour a light barge or skiff, manned by two sinewy blacks, might be seen darting from the shore, and clearing its way gracefully through the waters despite the powerful current which opposed its progress. Besides the rowers, a third person occupied a place in the boat, who appeared in the capacity of helmsman or guide. This person was Rosalind.

Our limited disclosures have already acquainted the reader with the fact that there existed a latent connection between this unprincipled profligate and the unfortunate child who had been committed for his crime : and, unwilling as we are to anticipate the regular developments of our narrative, we cannot suppress the observation that it was this hidden relation which tortured and perplexed the monster at this time. It seemed as if external objects conspired with his exasperated fancy, to enhance the deep despondency which, in spite of his indomitable energies, was fast diffusing itself throughout his heart. For years that heart had been as the mountain's icy coronal, which not even the seething rays of a meridian's sun can soften or dissolve. But the inevitable period had at length arrived when guilt can no longer withstand the power of remorse, and the black tyrant, with ruffled pinions and expanding claws, swoops higher in his flight, to pounce with accelerated velocity upon his prey. We have said that, notwithstanding the excessive agitation of his feelings, his intellect was calm and unconquered. Indeed its vigour might be said to have increased, if the last recuperative effort of despair may be so termed which prompted the ambitious Roman to think of decency in death, and stimulated the hero of Gaza to sacrifice the prospect of an ignominious existence, to the glory of a great revenge.

Impelled by the muscular strength of the two blacks, the diminutive bark glided swiftly across the river, towards the opposite point; and, in a few moments, the rowers, after a final stroke, uplifted their dripping oars, leaving it to drift, with slackened speed, to the neighbouring bank. The landing-place or quay, to which they now arrived, was situated at the foot of a steep elevation, being one of a small ridge of low hills that, at that time, extended along the margin of the river in a north-westerly direction from Charleston, and the traces of which may be seen to this day.

The skiff had no sooner touched the landing-place than Rosalind started up abruptly from his seat, and hurriedly stepped ashore.

"Secure it to the snag," he said, addressing one of the domestics by name, and pointing to an old stump which protruded upwards some two feet from the ground, and which, if a thick iron hoop attached to one side might be considered authority, appeared to be employed in ordinary for the purpose to which it was now applied. Without allowing them time to fulfil his order, he instructed them to keep within ear-shot of this spot during the whole day, and night, he added, in the event of his failing to be there at its close; an injunction which he deemed it advisable to accompany with sundry emphatic adjectives and formidable threats, that fully convinced the blacks a non-compliance with its requirements would be severely visited on the delinquent. Then drawing the deep shaded folds of his cloak more closely around him, he proceeded with hasty and somewhat irregular strides towards a grove of straggling oaks, whose umbrageous foliage deepened the gloom of a marsh-grown fen, which lay at the distance of a few yards back of the hillock, and was speedily lost in their long and Titan-like shadows.

Rosalind had scarcely disappeared, when, leaving their dull charge to take care of itself, the fellow bondsmen betook themselves to a neighbouring grocery, where gentlemen of their order were supplied with refreshments at the moderate rate of six and a quarter cents per head.

At an early hour an immense concourse of persons might be seen assembled around the old court house. Among these the utmost excitement prevailed respecting the probable issue of little Nora's trial, which, it was conjectured, would take place that morning. But in this expectation they were destined to be disappointed. Matters of various and momentous importance engrossed the attention of the court during the whole day, and it was not until the slanting beams and lengthened shadows of evening indicated the sun's fast approaching decline, that the hapless maiden's case came next in order for investigation. It was estimated, however, of sufficient moment, to induce the court to delay its adjournment; a favour which was never accorded, save where the feelings of the judge and jury were warmly enlisted in the prisoner's behalf. The effect which this announcement produced upon the anxious multitude, both within and without the building, cannot be easily conceived. Some started up from their seats in their eager curiosity to behold the youthful prisoner, whom they expected would be presently ushered into the stall; others, more earnestly concerned in her tender years and probable innocence than the exaggerated rumours which were circulated of her personal beauty, gave audible vent to their feelings in loud clamours, that the peremptorily commands of the officers could scarcely suppress; while a distracting and confused sound of mingled oaths and expostulations marked the impatience of the vast assemblage without, which, like a troubled sea, after the convulsive action of a recent tempest, heaved to and fro, in the restless intensity of popular ferment and commotion. But the damsel's name was no sooner called, in order that her arraignment might proceed, than the agitated mass were instantaneously reduced to order, and the dizzy hum of their conflicting voices subsided into a few incoherent whispers, which were gradually lost in an awful pause of breathless attention and profound silence. It was then, that the maiden, accompanied by her guardian, appeared at the threshold of a small side-door, through which the criminals were usually admitted into the hall. She leaned somewhat heavily upon his arm, and if her exterior person, which, naturally fragile, was now additionally weak and emaciated, might be assumed as a criterion of her feelings, indispensably required the support thus afforded her. Her languid black eyes were raised for an instant on

THE LANDING ON THE BANKS OF THE ASHLEY.

[The skiff had no sooner reached the landing-place, than Rosalind started up abruptly from his seat, and hurriedly stepped ashore.]

the motionless mass before her, as she timidly faltered and paused at the doorway; and the more humane of the audience at once observed that they were swollen and red with the humid traces of recent tears. Some, too, there were, who were moved to compassion by the deathly pallor of her complexion, which, spiritualized by the touch of adversity, was now invested with an expression of angelic purity and resignation, that the most hardened hearts found it difficult to withstand. It may be that her raven locks and sable apparel tended rather to increase than diminish the effect to which we allude; and though the excited imagination of the spectator may also have contributed much to produce it, there were few, nevertheless, who beheld her at this moment, that did not see, or fancy they saw, a luminous halo streaming around her brow, like that with which the limner encircles the celestial creations of his pencil.

She proceeded slowly to the criminal's box or stand, on being motioned to it by one of the officers in attendance, and, upon reaching its conspicuous platform, which was attained by means of a dilapidated flight of steps, paused breathless from exertion and flushed by the sense of her unmerited disgrace. Embarrassed and confused by the novelty of his situation, and deeply absorbed in sympathizing with the unfortunate maiden, Mr. Merrygold was on the eve of ascending the platform and sharing the odium of her more exalted position, when a subordinate officer interposed, and mildly suggested to him the informality of such a course.

It was now time for the prisoner to select the twelve jurors who should decide on the merits of her case, or, as the formula is more technically described, to challenge the array. They were, accordingly, produced, one after another, and made to confront her, after the customary form.

Eleven persons had thus passed her inspection, and been constituted her legal jurors:— there was but one more to be drawn. It may appear strange, but there stole over her mind at this moment a secret presentiment of impending danger, which seemed to un- bend every mental energy, and bade fair to crush the little fortitude which had, until then, sustained her. Under the pressure of this sudden impulse, she shrunk slightly back, as if to widen the distance that intervened betwixt her and the speaker, and, in some sort, to exclude her hearing from the awful sound, which was destined so speedily to reach it. But this was impossible; and, in tones whose distinctness seemed to her almost piercing, the clerk's lips slowly articulated the dreaded name—Philip Rosalind! At these words, her ears tingled with a burning sensation, and her heart's pulse throbbed full and fast, as the quick strokes of a broken pendulum ere its internal machinery ceases to revolve. She felt like one temporarily deafened by some sharp and unex- pected sound, and, such was the bewilderment of her mind and senses, that she did not observe the dark form which had instantaneously responded to the summons.

Rosalind had stepped forward from an inmost recess of the irregular chamber, where he was hitherto concealed from her sight, if, indeed, her mind had been collected enough to observe him, and now stood forth, enveloped in his muffling mantle, like the sheeted phantom, which the Sorceress of Endor evoked within her mystic ring—pale and frowning.

"Prisoner," said the clerk, solemnly; "look at the juryman."

She heard the words, and mechanically complied with their meaning, for her eyes saw nothing but a dim and a vascillating scene of objects apparently inverted and confused.

"Juryman, look at the prisoner," continued the speaker, turning towards Rosalind as he spoke; but the latter still kept his sombre glance fixed upon the ground, as if it were riveted there by some potent spell or absorbing fascination. A few seconds passed, and the clerk emphatically repeated the injunction.

"*I am,*" muttered a hoarse and troubled voice in reply, which would scarcely have been recognised for that of Rosalind, while he raised his half-closed eyelids upon the prisoner, and so changed in mien and colour when they met her's, that he resembled an abstract impersonation of the dreadful guilt, on which he was shortly to sit in judgment. On the other hand, the maiden retained the position into which her sudden apprehensions had thrown her ; and with one foot partially advanced, and the other half-withdrawn, her snowy fingers relaxed and drooping, her lovely face tinged with a sickly flush, and her small rosy lips parted with dismay, appeared, by the bright light of a globular lantern which was suspended above her, like an animated statue of the beautiful Daphne, represented, as she paused, fluctuating between fear and fatigue, in the assiduous pursuit of the day-god.

These tokens of alarm on the part of little Nora, together with the visible embarrassment of Rosalind, were, however, equally mistaken and misconstrued by the court, who ascribed the agitation of the first to her deplorable situation, while they imagined the other's discomposure to proceed from the laudable emotions of a good heart. Indeed, these ideas had prevailed so universally, that but few decided the latter's behaviour deserving of minute observation, and the clerk himself, mistaking little Nora's murmured rejection of the candidate for an expression of acquiescence, gravely proceeded to qualify him for the office.

As soon as the jurors, being sworn, were established in their respective places, the prosecuting attorney commenced to read her indictment aloud, which the grand jury had reluctantly sanctioned as a true bill, after rigidly examining the two rustics, whose depositions had led to her arrest and confinement. This done, the prisoner was directed to rise from her seat, while the clerk propounded to her the formal question, " Guilty, or not guilty ?" " Not guilty !" she replied, in a voice which, though soft and melodious, was singularly firm for so young a person, and which seemed to carry along with it that internal evidence of its own truth which the language of innocence is reputed to bear.

One after another the rustics were produced upon the stand, and severely cross-examined, afterwards, as to the matter which their testimony unfolded in the examination in chief. Next came the evidence on the part of the prisoner, which was chiefly concerning her general character and local reputation. This last was of the highest and most favourable nature, and furnished a conclusive argument to many of the more humane of the audience, who, in their zeal to defend her from the imputation of crime, had boldly ventured on *a priori* inferences, drawn from the guileless purity of her manner, and the matchless loveliness of her person.

The attorney-general rose slowly from his seat, and solemnly addressed the court. He briefly adverted to the deep excitement which the case had universally produced ; and, after describing the emotions of sorrow and trepidation with which he entered on the responsible duties of his office, proceeded to analyse the testimony adduced. He dwelt on her strange abandonment of Mr. Merrygold's mansion, during the stormy night in which the atrocious deed was committed—spoke of the misunderstanding and ill-feeling that Lucy's obstruction to the little girl's design when used as a messenger by the two lovers, had generated—coloured every trivial incident of the prisoner's mien and manner during their habitual intercourse, with the hues of malignity and revenge—till, in short, as a skilful fowler ensnares his unwary prey with slow but unerring certainty, he dashed, with gloomy and fearful pencil, on the frontispiece of his appalling picture, the fatal circumstance of her condition when discovered in the morning. The wan corpse —the dripping knife—the streaming gash, all were painted with such blood-congealing fidelity, that the horror-struck maiden felt her heart grow faint, and her limbs give way beneath her, and the fickle mob, who, a moment before, would have rushed to her rescue, now moved, and muttered darkly in their seats—like the drowsy roar of a slumbering lion.

"Oh, God !" Nora fervently exclaimed, in the artless simplicity of her young heart, "thou hast left no father or mother to thy little child, but thou art alike a parent to all, and wilt deign to hear a friendless orphan's supplication, in this her hour of peril and affliction !"   This earnest invocation, whispered softly to herself, by the young girl, was yet fresh from her lips, when a faint and far distant hum dawned, as it were, upon the ear from the farthermost extremity of the multitude without, which, barely perceptible at first, swept hoarsely onward like a rising blast—swelling second after second into deeper distinctness—till a deafening peal of simultaneous voices shook the gothic window panes of the building with violence, and its shivering echoes sullenly reverberated the awful words,—" A witness !—a witness !—a witness !"

Almost at the same instant a sudden and crushing movement was made by the vast assemblage, and the people, eagerly clambering upon one another's shoulders, in utter recklessness of personal comfort or safety, separated themselves in two huge masses, or piles of human shapes, as the waters of the Red Sea, when their heaving billows divided at the prophet's command.   Through the narrow avenue or vista thus formed, which extended far beyond the portals of the court into the open air, two figures might now be partially discerned, rapidly advancing towards the hall.   One of these was a young and well-built man, who, in his anxiety to reach the place, carelessly dragged his companion after him, an aged woman of low and bending frame, habited in black, whose face was screened from observation by a veil of the same dark hue.   All these circumstances transpired in the space of an instant, and the next saw Edward St. Julian and the house-keeper Lucy, standing mute and breathless from exertion within the precincts of the court.

If the heavy arches and cross-beams of the massive building, and the firmly cemented stones of which it was composed, had, at this moment, burst their inseparable conjunction, and, crumbling to earth, left Rosalind unimpaired in life or limb, his features could not have revealed a more faithful expression of mingled horror and amazement than they now presented.   He bounded up from his place, and, incoherently muttering the names of St. Julian and Lucy, stood up, stiff and motionless, as if every portion of his frame had been suddenly petrified.

For several seconds the guilty man continued in the erect posture which his body had involuntarily assumed ; then smiling darkly, while his rolling eyes sparkled with that fearful brilliancy so peculiar to madness, he drew from his vest a folded paper, and, pointing to a written inscription upon it, exultingly observed, "You see ! there—there ! is it not ?   Ha ! ha ! thou need'st not have come from thy dotard's grave with those red spots upon thee !" and, suddenly imagining (for no one moved or spoke, such was the all-absorbing interest of the spectators) that he was about to be secured, he tore open his vest, and grasped a pistol.   A sharp report rung through the apartment, and a disfigured and bleeding corpse tumbled headlong from the spot, where, a second before, the darkling dreams of insanity had breathed into Philip Rosalind's guilty soul and yet conscious frame a foretaste of his eternal destiny.

A brief explanation is perhaps due to the reader, that he may become acquainted with the circumstances which occasioned the sudden appearance of Edward St. Julian in court, with the old beldame, whose return to the world, from which he firmly believed her to have departed, excited such deep consternation in the schoolmaster's mind. After their amusing interview, she was transferred by the latter, in compliance with her own instructions, to his home, where the money she had prudently secreted on her person procured her the double advantage of remedies for her wound and obedience to her commands. There she remained concealed until the day on which little Nora's trial was expected to take place, when she despatched a hasty message to Edward St. Julian, requesting a personal conference immediately on matters of pressing importance. He accordingly attended, and the result of this unexpected rencontre between two persons, of whom one, at least, never entertained a hope, however faint or distant, of again beholding the other, has been unfolded in the stirring scene which we have so imperfectly described.

We must further observe, that the confession prepared by Rosalind as a *dernier resort* to rescue Little Nora from being ignominiously punished for a crime which he imagined himself to have succeeded in committing, contained, besides a minute account of his past career, many startling revelations of fact strictly essential to the proper understanding of our narrative.

It would appear from this paper, that after betraying Adrian St. Julian, the bosom friend and companion of his youth, and consummating the poor girl's ruin, to whom the last had sacrificed his most cherished projects and noblest affections, he abandoned South Carolina, and sheltered himself from the vengeance of his injured associate in the household of a wealthy relation, residing in Georgia. Here he persisted in his illicit intercourse with the helpless victim of his duplicity under the specious veil of a past matrimonial alliance; and here, also, it was that he became acquainted and leagued in unlawful confederacy with the wily Italian, who then belonged to one of the countless bands of outlaws and pirates that infested the waters of the Ashley, and who afterwards exerted so unpropitious an influence upon his fortunes. It was here, in short, that his dark and designing mind first grew familiar with the horrid thought of depriving a fellow-creature of life, and that he learnt to regard it with the callous hardihood of habitual crime.

On reaching his uncle's mansion, where he was most cordially received, he found that the latter was recently married to a young and blooming country maiden, who had cheerfully sacrificed the dawning glories of her spinsterhood to the prospect of rank and affluence, which the alliance promised; though these goods were, in her case, lucklessly united to that worst of all plagues, an aged and doting husband.

A year after Rosalind's arrival, his uncle's youthful consort bade fair to increase the matrimonial joys of her household. The blissful event had been long eagerly anticipated, and the period now approached when its realisation might be daily expected. About this time, Rosalind's supposed wife was also in momentary anticipation of a similar, but to her sinful and sorrowing heart, much less joyful occurrence. The event arrived simultaneously for both—but with far different success. The first did not survive the agonies of travail, and expired in the very instant which imparted life and light to her child. The latter was most fortunate, and gave birth to a healthy infant, whose incipient features even then gave promise of rivalling her mother's, in symmetry and loveliness, at no distant day.

It was at this moment, while the mourning drapery of the hearse temporarily superseded and darkened the sunny serenity of the cradle—and the fond father was forgotten in the bereaved husband, that Rosalind's foul purposes, so long retarded by the lack of a fitting occasion, expanded into their fullest maturity.

The funeral rites proceeded; the hollow bell tolled the solemn knell of the departed; and while the bier was being lowered to its final home, the wily nephew might be seen, earnestly pressing the chief mourner's hand, and apparently striving to solace and console his deep affliction. Who, of the vast and sorrowing multitude, which was then collected, would have surmised, that those eyes, now beaming with compassion, would look unmoved, ere the dawn, upon a corpse?—or that that outstretched hand, whose fervent grasp spoke more eloquently still the language of sympathy and regret, could bear, at midnight, the assassin's torch and steel to the couch of a benefactor? Yet such were the base designs of this abandoned wretch; and the same clear blue night, whose azure 'curtains silently closed around the wife's newly-made grave, beheld, by the pallid light of its vigiling spheres, the foul massacre of her husband.

This done, there was but one frail barrier left between the murderer's grasping avarice and the wealth he had so long secretly coveted. This obstacle was his infant cousin. Through the agency of Lucy, who had, during her illness, constantly attended upon his aunt, in the capacity of a professional midwife, a report of its death was circulated, while the child was given to his paramour, upon whom he strictly enjoined to conceal her own, in order that the deception might be safely practised on the public. But the latter had suffered too much and too long from her first criminal step to bear any addition to the burden of woe under which she laboured; and, a week after this terrible catastrophe, she fled, with her child, a raving maniac, from the arms of a profligate and the homestead of an assassin. Rosalind removed, shortly afterwards, to South Carolina, where he continued to reside till the period at which our tale commences, alternately tortured by the bitterness of his own reflections, and that restless fear of exposure and punishment which is ever present to a guilty mind.

CHAPTER XXI.

CONCLUSION.

A YEAR had transpired since the incidents we have endeavoured to transcribe in the foregoing pages. A cloudless morning was mirrored in the smooth, blue waters of the Ashley, which, like a sheet of burnished gold, glittered in the dazzling sunlight. Lawn and meadow, dingle and hill, displayed the rich luxuriance of spring, and its thousand warblers were abroad, chanting merrily their sylvan notes of rejoicing and praise. This day had been appointed to celebrate the union of our hero with Blanche.

The ceremony was over, and the happy couple, prompted by a natural wish to muse among the solitudes of nature, and to revive those brilliant associations of the past, which their checkered fortunes had only tended to enliven and endear, directed their buoyant steps to the mystic ruins, where, of yore, they secretly repaired to whisper the hopes and projects of affection, and to commune, as love communes, unseen and unheard!

"It has come, at length, my dear Blanche!" exclaimed the bridegroom, folding her tenderly to his bosom,—"that day, so wished for,—so delayed! My own, my lovely wife!" And the bride did not avert her joyful glance, as he imprinted on her lips the fervent signet of his unspeakable felicity.

So ends our tale.

www.ingramcontent.com/pod-product-compliance
Lightning Source LLC
Chambersburg PA
CBHW081212170626
46811CB00010B/3253